The Magical
Matchmaker's Legacy

THE CONALL'S MAGICAL YULETIDE

USA TODAY BESTSELLING AUTHOR
BETHANY CLAIRE

A NOVELLA

Copyright 2017 by Bethany Claire
All rights reserved.

License Notes

All rights reserved. This book or any portion thereof may not be reproduced or used in any manner whatsoever without the express written permission of the author except for the use of brief quotations in a book review.

This story is a work of fiction. Names, characters, places, and incidents are either products of the author's imagination or used fictitiously. Any resemblance to actual events, locales, or persons, living or dead, is entirely coincidental.

Editor: J.J. Archer
Cover Designed by Sarah Hansen, Okay Creations

Available In eBook & Paperback

eBook ISBN: 978-1-947731-01-1
Paperback ISBN: 978-1-947731-02-8
Hardback ISBN: 978-1-947731-03-5

http://www.bethanyclaire.com

AUTHOR NOTE

AUTHOR NOTE: "The Conall's Magical Yuletide" is the SWEET/CLEAN version of "A Conall Christmas," originally published in 2013 by Bethany Claire.

CHAPTER 1

*C*onall Castle, Scotland - December 1646

There's nothing quite like the soft thump on your palm as you press it against a swollen, pregnant belly, allowing the small infant tucked safely away in its mother's womb to kick at the inside of your hand. The surreal experience filled me with joy as I pressed my hands flush against my daughter's stomach, smiling widely as tears brimmed in my eyes. I'd felt the child's movement more than once, but it didn't matter. I had the same reaction every time. My baby's baby had completely captured my heart, even if it would still be weeks before I would know she could be safely delivered without the conveniences of technology and medicine from our own time.

"All right, Mom. You simply cannot keep your hands glued to my stomach every moment of every day."

I smiled as Bri stepped away, grabbing the end of the blanket and tossing the other end in my direction, signaling for me to help fold it. "Oh, but I wish that I could. I think the babe moves even more than you did, dear, and you were quite active."

"Really? Well, I sincerely apologize. I'm beginning to feel miserable."

As if to emphasize her point, she collapsed onto her freshly-made bed and threw her hands up over her head as far as her dress would allow. I kicked off my own shoes, hiking up my dress as I sat crisscrossed on the end of the bed. Pulling Bri's legs across my lap, I removed her shoes so I could massage her swollen, most-assuredly sore, feet.

She sighed, wiggling her toes as I squeezed them, and I suddenly saw her as the little girl she'd once been. She was more than ready and capable of taking care of a child, but I found it hard to believe she'd grown so quickly, and that I was old enough to be a grandmother.

I continued to knead the arches of her feet and heels until she drifted off to sleep. When she began to snore lightly, I carefully lifted her legs so that I could scoot out from under them, and crawled off the bed as gently as I could. I walked to the fireplace, poking the logs until the flame took a firm root over them once more. I curled into a small wooden chair that sat before the blaze, gazing first into the flames before glancing about the room.

Every inch of the castle oozed magic. I sensed it in the air. As I sat with the fire warming my bare toes, I could almost feel Morna's eyes watching over us across the centuries.

No surprise, really. I imagined it only made sense that magic be palpable throughout the castle. Magic had, after all, brought both Bri and me to live in this place and century when we'd been born hundreds of years in the future.

Before my trip into the past, I'd been an archaeologist who specialized in Celtic finds and history. The Conall Clan was my specialty, the last twenty plus years of my life spent trying to solve the mystery behind who'd murdered them in December of 1645.

My continuing efforts to solve this mystery brought my daughter and me to the ruins of Conall Castle only one year ago, in the year 2013. I'd pestered her until she'd agreed to accompany me, not knowing that a spell cast by a beloved Conall ancestor, Morna, would rip Bri from our time and bring her into the past to live with the Conalls right before the devastating massacre was supposed to take place.

Thankfully, Bri was meant to be here. Not only did she help them change the course of history by stopping the massacre, but she also fell in love with the man of her dreams, Conall Castle's new laird, Eoin. I'd been unwilling to be separated from my daughter, no matter how happy I was for her. So when Bri decided to stay in this time with her husband, I used Morna's spell to travel back to the seventeenth century, as well.

The greatest dream of an archaeologist's life is to live with the very people he or she has devoted so much of a lifetime to learn about. And I now lived that dream-like existence. However, it was slowly becoming a reality I accepted. On top of it all, I would soon become a grandma.

I was as happy as I'd ever been, with only one lingering thought keeping me from overwhelming joy. I'd always been a social person. I liked to date. I liked to flirt. While it had become more difficult to find a date with someone my age even in the twenty-first century, I was certain that in the seventeenth century men considered me hopelessly over-the-hill, with one foot deep into the grave.

I would most likely spend the rest of my days alone, something I'd realized shortly after arriving in this time, but a fact of life that took me a bit longer to accept than I had hoped.

No matter. I had much to be thankful for. Christmas time, my favorite time of the year, had arrived. I was anxious to discuss preparations for the holiday with Bri. So when I saw her stir, I stood from my place by the fire and went to her side.

"What?" I knew the pitch of my voice rose too high, almost to a squeak, but if that old bat thought she could stifle our Christmas, she had another think coming.

"Mom, is it really that big of a deal? We didn't even notice it last year."

The hormones were messing with Bri's head. She loved Christmas as much I did. I couldn't imagine how she seemed to be so fine with skipping Christmas. "Yes, it's that big of a deal! Of course you didn't notice it last year. You were all too busy trying to stop the attack on the castle. What's Mary's problem with Christmas?"

I didn't miss the look of frustration in Bri's eyes as she answered my question. "Mary likes Christmas very much. She loves cooking. You know that. It's only that after Eoin's mother passed away, Christmas became less of an event as the years went on. Not to mention, it's been outlawed in Scotland for the last four decades."

My expression mimicked my daughter's frustration. "Darling, you know as well as I do that Christmas continued to be celebrated, just a little more quietly. Besides, who is there to enforce it when your husband is laird?"

"Well...no one really. Look, I love Christmas, but I've no desire to put Mary into more of a tizzy than she stays in constantly. If you can get her to agree to it, then I will be the first to jump on the Christmas bandwagon with you."

"Oh, I'll get her to agree. As much as she likes to fight it, I'm Mary's closest friend, and she's all bark, anyhow. Go and get

Eoin. While I know that Mary will eventually get on board, we may need him to intervene in the argument she's sure to put up."

Bri nodded and laughed as I turned and left her bedchamber. This was no laughing matter. Whether the child was present or not, my first grandbaby would have a Christmas to rival any other. I would make certain of it.

CHAPTER 2

Three Days Ride North of Conall Castle

Snow built outside Hew's window, and his creaky joints told him a bad storm brewed. Still, he left his home at this time every year. He'd not missed his trip to her gravesite once in the twenty-plus years since his beloved had passed away. He did not intend to let the snow deter his plans.

Hew walked around his small home, tidying up before his journey south. He lived alone, far away from the nearest village. He'd not seen another soul in months, and that was just as he would have it. He knew his shyness held him back. It had been a wonder that he had ever married at all.

Hew had not expected it, the day his sister's best friend, Mae, had approached him while he chopped wood for the fire at the back of his family home, grabbing his face and kissing him squarely on the mouth. He'd been a young lad then, and that kiss had changed his life. Hew had grown up with Mae constantly underfoot, as she and his sister were inseparable. While he had silently admired her for many years before that kiss, he was far too shy to ever express the way his heart beat for her.

That night so many years ago, he'd felt her watching him, but did not turn to greet her. His heart pounded uncomfortably just having her near. He continued to swing his ax down into the blocks, swiftly chopping the wood into two pieces. Her hand on the lower part of his back caused him to jump, and he nicked the edge of the block of wood before he threw his ax to the ground and whirled to face her.

"Mae, ye startled me, lass. Ye should be inside. 'Tis far too cold for ye to be out of doors." He could remember every word spoken between them, the scene held captive forever in his mind.

She'd touched his arm then, smiling as she shook her head, dismissing his worry. "Hew, if 'tis not too cold for ye to be out here, then I doona think I shall freeze to death, either. Did ye know that I shall turn ten and eight tomorrow?"

He'd stepped away from her, too nervous to simply stand there with her hand lying on his arm. "Nay, lass. I dinna know. I shall make ye something. Carve ye a piece of jewelry, perhaps?" He didn't know what to say to her – never did.

"I would like that verra much, but that isna why I mentioned it to ye."

He'd gathered the freshly chopped logs of wood into his hands, desperate to keep busy in her presence. "Nay? Why did ye then?"

He stilled when she moved to stand in front of him, blocking his path. "Will ye set all that down for only a moment, Hew? I'm trying to talk to ye."

He reddened and obeyed. "Aye, lass. Why doona we sit for a moment?"

They'd moved to the pile of wood, stacked just high enough to serve as the perfect chair. He trembled as she grabbed his hands, but he swallowed his nerves and forced himself not to flinch away from her touch. "What is it, lass?"

"As I just told ye, I shall be ten and eight tomorrow, and I doona wish to become an old maid."

Hew couldn't still the twitch of his hand as he realized where she headed with her words. "Nay, lass, I doona believe ye will. There are many lads who would eagerly wed ye."

"Aye, I doona believe that I shall become an old maid, either. Still, most my age are already married. While yer sister is several years older than me, she was married at ten and seven. And ye are right, many lads would be willing to wed me, but I am not so eager to marry them."

"Why is that, lass? Is there no one that catches yer fancy?" It was too much for Hew to wish that Mae would answer as he wanted, but to his everlasting shock, she did.

"Aye, there is one, and I willna allow him a moment longer to behave as if he doesna care for me as much as I care for him."

His heart began to beat so quickly he feared she could feel its quick pulse in his fingertips. Though a cold night, sweat beaded freely on his brow. "Is that so, lass? And who is this lad ye speak of?"

"If ye doona know, ye are as daft as yer sister seems to think ye are."

She paused and reached in quickly to kiss him. He was so stunned, she pulled away before he could react and kiss her back properly. "Nay, lass. Ye canna mean it. 'Tis some other lad that ye mean and ye are simply using me for practice, aye?"

She laughed before kissing him again. This time he pulled her close as she melted against him. Breathlessly, she pulled away from him so she could whisper into his ear. "Nay, Hew, there is none other but ye. There never has been. Ye are going to marry me."

He smiled against her cheek, her confidence somehow diminishing his shyness. "If ye insist, lass."

"Aye, I do."

"And what shall ye do with me once we are married?" His hands found their way to her hair, and he cradled her against his chest, pulling her into a tight embrace.

"We shall move north, find a piece of land for only the two of us, and together we shall build a home where we will spend all of our days together."

They married within a fortnight and proceeded just as Mae had wished. After moving north, they built a home for the two of them, one isolated from the rest of humanity. Five years flew by in a haze of love in which they spent every moment at each other's side.

Eventually, they planned a trip to visit their families in Conall territory. They left in winter, and Mae fell ill on their journey. She fought hard, but the sickness was too much. She died only two days after they arrived at their destination. Hew chose to bury her there, at the place in which she'd grown up. Afterward, with a broken heart, he returned to their home alone.

Hew saddled his horse, pushing away the memories of his past as he headed out into the storm. It had been many years since Mae passed. While he would feel her absence always, his heart had now healed as much as it ever could from such a wrenching loss.

Each year, he continued to make the trip to her grave on the anniversary of her death. He did so to pay his respects, to speak to her, to remind himself that there was once a time in his life when he had not been so completely alone.

CHAPTER 3

Conall Castle

I tried to make as much noise as I could as I made my way downstairs into the castle's kitchen. I was certain Mary would be there, busily working away on the evening meal. I was right, and she instantly knew it was me creating the commotion.

"Adelle, ye doona always have to make such a ruckus when ye move about. Come in here and help me plate the food."

I knew I was normally no louder than anyone else in the castle, but Mary constantly looked for something to nag me about, so I obliged her by being purposely obnoxious in her presence.

In many ways, Mary was the castle's most important resident. She'd worked there for nearly forty years. Everyone, especially Eoin and his brother Arran, accepted the cook and head maid as the castle's true boss. She ran the castle like the captain of a ship.

Nothing happened within the walls without her notice or approval.

I stuck my head into the kitchen, smiling as I reached up onto the shelf just out of her reach to grab the plates. I thought it best to test her mood before immediately jumping into what I wanted to discuss with her. "How are you today, Mary?"

Mary motioned for me to lay out the plates, saying, "Ach, I'm fine. 'Tis a bonny day. I enjoy the snowfall, but I feel a bit of guilt for loving it so. 'Tis sure to mean more work for Kip in the stables to keep the horses warm."

"Oh, don't feel guilty about enjoying anything, Mary. You know that Eoin and Arran will both do whatever they need to do so that Kip's load in the stables is not more than he can handle. I have a wonderful idea that I think we should all consider doing together before the snow outside gathers too much."

"What might that be?"

"I think we should all go out and find a tree to cut down for Christmas." I looked down at the plates, busying my hands as I awaited her reaction. Perhaps if I pretended I didn't know her thoughts on the matter, she would be more willing to discuss it.

Mary turned away to grab the bread, and then began breaking it into pieces. "Nay, I'm afraid 'tis not possible. Lovely thought, though."

In the year that I'd known her, Mary had never referred to anything I'd ever said as "lovely." I was unsure of how to respond. "Umm...why 'tis not possible?"

She didn't appreciate my attempt to mimic her accent. Casting a frown at me, she said, "Well, Christmas is no longer openly celebrated in Scotland, and after Elspeth passed away, Alasdair dinna find the joy in the season he once did. The two lads dinna grow up with it being a grand celebration."

"Do you not enjoy Christmas yourself, Mary?" Eoin and Arran's history with Christmas seemed irrelevant. Alasdair had been dead for over a year, and I couldn't imagine either of his sons having a problem with the festivities. Their mother had died when they were very young. While Christmas might have brought up painful memories for their father, it would not have the same effect on either of them.

Mary shook her head and returned to help me with the plating of our meal. "Nay, lass. I enjoyed Christmas verra much when I was a young girl. My brother always made me the most beautiful presents. He was quite the craftsman."

"Mary." Her words surprised me. "I didn't know you had a brother. Is he…is he still living?"

"Aye lass, verra much so, but I doona see him often. He lives far away from here and is a bit shy. Always had a difficult time interacting with others. Only certain people had the ability to draw him out."

She looked down, as if saddened by some memory. I interrupted her thoughts to try and lift the mood. "Are you certain he's related to you? How could one sibling end up so shy while the other does nothing but talk?"

Mary rewarded me with a quick whack on the arm as she chuckled and resumed her work in the kitchen. "Aye, I'm certain. I suppose he was shy because I never gave him much of a chance to speak. As he grew, he simply grew accustomed to his own silence."

I couldn't help but wonder about Mary's brother, about her family, and what she would have been like as a child. I felt close to my dear friend now, but I honestly knew very little about her. She was always so busy caring for everyone else that I feared we often forgot about the woman within her. I shook my head, remembering my reason for speaking with her. "You have very cleverly changed the subject, Mary. If you enjoy Christmas, then why are you against us celebrating it? I'm sure you have some wonderful traditions you could share with us, and Bri and I could share ours with all of you, as well."

Mary tried to hide the smile that pulled at the corners of her mouth, but I could sense her resolve dropping.

"I'll not say that it wouldna be a pleasant time. I just doona wish to upset the laddies if 'tis something that should bring up memories of their parents."

A deep voice in the doorway caused us both to turn our heads. I smiled as Eoin and Bri poked their heads into the kitchen. Eoin's strong hands rested gently on Bri's shoulders as she leaned the back of her head lovingly into his chest. "It will do no such thing, Mary. Ma made Yuletide a spectacle and, while Da did try, it wasna the same after she passed. I think 'tis far past time for us to restore the celebrations to their former glory."

Mary let her smile pull free now, and I could see that the idea excited her.

"If that is what ye want, my dear lad, then I shall be as pleased as anyone. I only dinna want to upset ye or Arran."

Eoin moved across the room, each step accentuating his strength. His hair was even darker than Bri's, his eyes the color of obsidian glass. My grandchild was going to be beautiful.

He wrapped his arm around Mary, drawing her near before bending to kiss her on the cheek. "Aye, I know. Ye are always watching out for us, and I love ye for it, Mary."

He released her and stepped away to regard us. "Do ye think the two of ye can work together to make the preparations?"

I smiled, bobbing my head up and down enthusiastically. "Of course we can." I could sense that Mary was about to intercede with some jab as to how difficult it would be for her to put up with me, so I quickly added, "Do we have permission to do whatever we wish?" I already had a grand idea, but I didn't want to mention it to anyone before I'd convinced Mary.

Eoin grinned and glanced cautiously at Bri. "I feel that I may come to regret this but, aye, I shall not tell either of ye lassies what to do. It would be wrong of me to do so, and it would be a fruitless effort anyway."

"Absolutely right." I scooted over and draped an arm around Mary's shoulder. She glared up at me in response. "Don't you two worry. Mary and I are going to make certain this is the most magnificent Christmas Conall Castle has ever seen."

CHAPTER 4

"Adelle, ye have lost yer mind if ye believe for one moment that I would do such a foolish thing as follow ye into that God-forsaken time that ye came from!"

Listening to Mary rant, I crossed my arms and sat down on the steps leading down into the castle's basement and spell room. It was impossible for her first reaction to anything that came out of my mouth to be a positive one.

"What is so important that ye would feel the need to do such a thing? I know ye are daft, but gracious, 'tis a horrible idea. What if we were unable to return home? I doona think I could stand to spend one day there."

"Calm down, Mary," I said, deciding it was time to intercede before her head exploded. "Morna's spells are reliable. Now that we know she lives in the inn near the castle, we will go straight there to stay with her. You don't even have to go into Edinburgh with me if you don't wish to. Wouldn't you like to see Morna again?"

Mary's face changed from red to white much too quickly. I was afraid I was about to have to pick her up off the ground. She extended a shaky hand in my direction, letting it hang in front of my face at eye level. "Do ye see what ye do to me? Ye have me so upset, I shall not stop shaking for days. Nay, I doona wish to see Morna again. The lass was a dear friend, but I spent the last twenty-five years believing her dead. 'Tis where the dead should stay. Good and buried."

Breathless, she plopped down next to me. I reached out to pat her on the back but quickly retracted my hand in response to the daggers her gray eyes shot toward me. "She was never dead, Mary. She just moved on to a different time. I'm sure she would love to see you."

"Nay, I doona expect she wishes to see me that much. If she did, could she not just come here herself to visit?"

I shook my head, regretting the direction I'd led our conversation. I didn't know enough about Morna or her abilities to speak of her so freely. "Nevermind. Don't go for Morna. Go for me. Surely you wouldn't want me to travel there alone?"

I was none too worried about going alone. I'd lived my entire life, for the most part, alone. It would be no problem for me to make the journey to my own time without anyone along. But the temptation of watching rigid, uptight Mary in the twenty-first century was a joy I very much wanted to gift to myself. It would be the best Christmas present I could ask for.

"I doona give two twiddles whether ye go alone. I hope that ye go and get stuck there. Can ye not tell by now that I'm not that fond of ye?"

I smirked at her jab. I spent most of every day at her side. If she truly didn't enjoy my company, I knew her well enough to know that she wouldn't put up with my presence. "Hush, Mary. If you're really so afraid to go along, that's all you had to say. I wouldn't have pressed you further. It's not good for someone your age to upset yourself and get so stressed out." I winked at her. "You're much too old to let fear overwhelm you." Mary was only a few years older than me, but I liked to pretend she was much, much older.

Mary stood abruptly and stomped her foot like a small child. "'Tis not that I'm frightened, only that ye are foolish to do so."

"I'll make you a deal, Mary. If you go, I'll help you with whatever chore you wish for the next month."

Mary hated, more than anything, beating the bed linens. I could already see her wrestling with the temptation of my offer in the way her eyes darted back and forth, calculating the pros versus the cons of saying yes. Eventually her eyes stopped moving, and she said, "Aye, fine, but I willna wear breeches that go up between my legs. I shall be allowed to stay in my dress the whole time, or I will not agree to go with ye."

I smiled. "Deal. You will look ridiculous, but it doesn't matter to me one bit as long as you come. Let's go tell Bri and then be on our way."

Present Day

Bri had warned me that, with the castle no longer in ruins as it had been when I lived in the twenty-first century, the site had become a popular tourist attraction. Still, I had underestimated the number of people that might be milling around when Mary and I arrived.

We made it out of the roped-off basement undetected, but the stares Mary's clothing garnered as we made our way were enough to rival an eight-legged horse at a zoo. Luckily, Mary was so bug-eyed at everything she saw that she remained completely oblivious to the pointing fingers and stares.

Once outside, we began the long walk to the inn. "Excuse my language, Adelle, but holy bugger," said Mary. "My head hurts something awful. I knew that it would from witnessing both Bri and yerself come through, but I dinna expect it to be quite so bad."

I winced. "Yes, I'm sorry. Morna will have something we can take to get rid of the pain. I'm certain of it." I tilted my head, studying her expression as we walked. "What do you think so far?" I asked.

"Well, I was surprised to find the castle looking much the same. But 'tis lighted much more, and oddly."

"Yes, electricity is amazing. All homes and buildings have it."

"Is that so?" Mary took in the scenery around us. "As we walk along this path, it doesna look so different."

She was right; besides the gravel road leading to the castle, this part of Scotland was still very much untouched by the conveniences of modern times. "Yes, unless you decide to accompany me into Edinburgh, your shocks will be less than they could be. Morna's home will have many things to surprise you, but nothing like the city."

"Aye, well I canna say that I doona enjoy the adventure of it. Perhaps I *will* join ye when ye leave for the city."

We walked in silence for the remainder of the way until we arrived at Jerry and Morna's. I was none too surprised to find both of them waiting for us at the front door.

"Ach, Mary!" Morna exclaimed. "I canna believe it! I nearly spit up my food when my vision showed me yesterday morning that ye two lassies were on yer way to see us."

Morna charged Mary, who blanched at the shock of laying eyes on the dear friend she'd thought lost forever. The two pulled each other into a tight embrace.

Jerry made his way over to me, then wrapped his rail-thin arms around my neck. "Adelle, it is lovely to see ye again, lass."

"You as well, Jerry. So, Morna saw us coming?"

Morna's voice answered me as she and Mary walked toward us, arm-in-arm. "Aye, I did. And I've not been so pleased by a vision in some time. I'm also thrilled to know that our dear Bri is with child, is she not?"

"Yes, and she's close to popping. Only a few more weeks, and my grandchild will make its appearance. I simply cannot wait." I smiled, leaning in to give Morna my hug of greeting.

Morna waved us inside her home. "I'm sure 'tis true, lass. I have something I wish for ye to take back with ye. It's an herbal potion I've mixed. 'Twill help her greatly with the pains of labor."

"Oh, thank you so much. I've been worrying myself sick thinking about the ordeal that's ahead of her. I thought I was going to die when I gave birth to Bri, and I let them drug me up with every medicine they had."

Morna laughed as we made our way into the sitting room. Mary's eyes bulged at the sight of every odd trinket. When Morna pointed at a box in the corner, tears immediately filled my eyes.

"I also retrieved something else for ye, lass," Morna said.

I had to keep from running toward the large box of ornaments, each a special memory of the Christmases Bri and I had spent together while she was growing up. Every year our collection grew, and each new ornament was a new, precious memory. "Morna!" I hadn't a clue how to express my gratitude.

"'Tis what ye really wanted, is it not?"

I nodded in disbelief. "Yes, but it never crossed my mind that I would actually be able to get them. I just planned to go into Edinburgh and buy a brand new set. All of this was in the States, at Bri's old place. How did you...how did you do this?"

She laughed heartily. "Did I not just make it possible for the two of ye to come here from hundreds of years in the past? Compared to that, 'twas a simple task to move these to us. Look in the other box. I also included a few other things I could sense were precious to ye."

My hands trembled with excitement as I moved to open the lid of the next box. I opened it to find an old CD player that could be operated with large DD batteries, packs and packs of replacement batteries, and our entire collection of Christmas music. Bri's baby blanket, knitted by my own mother, gently padded the Christmas items. Tears fell freely at the sight of it. "Oh my God, Morna. Are you a mind reader, as well?"

Jerry interjected playfully, "Aye, she is lass, and 'tis terribly annoying. I canna silently begrudge her anything without her finding out about it and charming me into forgiving her."

Morna laughed and leaned gently into her husband. "I am not that good at it, but ye are quite open with yer thoughts. 'Twas easy to see the things ye desired most from your trip here."

She was spot on. There was nothing more that I wished to retrieve. Everything I thought I would be unable to find was here. As far as I was concerned, we could make our way back to the castle immediately. But as I glanced over to see Mary in the kitchen, gleefully playing with the running water coming from the faucet, I thought better of suggesting we leave right away. "I cannot thank you enough, Morna. There's no need for me to make a trip into the city now, but would it be all right with you if we stay here tonight and leave in the morning?"

"Of course, lass. I wouldna have it any other way. I'm anxious to catch up with Mary, and I canna wait to hear her cries of excitement when we allow her to take a hot shower."

CHAPTER 5

*N*ear Conall Castle - 1646

The wind blew icy snow roughly into his face, and Hew could barely see the path in front of him. His fingers and nose burned from the pain of the harsh wind and bitter cold. With each step forward, his horse slowed his pace.

He didn't wish to stop for the night. He was so very close to the end of his journey, but he knew that his four-legged companion would not be able to go much further. He groaned at the thought of where he knew he must stop—Conall Castle—his sister's place of residence. The castle was so close that he could make out the silhouette of it in the distance, its grandness evident even through the storm.

It had been far too long since Hew had paid a visit to Mary. Nearly ten years by his count, possibly longer. He missed his sister, but he knew she would treat his arrival as a celebration, and the thought of such attention caused him to cringe inwardly.

Still, there was hardly another choice. Bracing himself for the torture he knew was about to ensue, he leaned down close to Greggory's ear, whispering words of encouragement as he nudged the old horse to the right. "Just a wee bit further, lad. There shall be a fine stable and blankets to keep ye warm just ahead. I'm sorry to have taken ye out in such a storm. I shall see ye well fed tonight, old fellow."

Flames flickered in the stables, so Hew knew before he approached that someone was still at work within them. They were most likely preparing the horses for the evening, making sure they were properly tended to in the cold weather.

He rode straight into the stables without seeking permission. He knew enough of the Conalls' generosity to know that they would not protest anyone seeking shelter for their horse on such a night.

Hew dismounted, quickly brushing the snow off of Greggory's coat, jumping at the sound of the voice in the far-end stall. "What sort of a fool would travel in this weather? 'Tis not so good for yer horse, sir. What be yer name?"

Hew's cheeks suddenly warmed. For a moment, he feared he would be unable to utter a word. He'd not spoken to another person in many moons. He swallowed, steeling himself for the task. "The fool's name is Hew. I apologize for the intrusion, but I must ask yer permission to allow me and my horse to rest here for the night. The poor lad willna be able to go much further."

A strong man as tall as him, with long, shaggy blond hair stepped out of the stall and smiled as he walked toward him. He knew it must be the youngest Conall brother, Arran, but the lad had been much younger when last Hew had seen him.

"Aye, of course ye can. It would be a wretched man to turn away anyone in a storm such as this."

Hew continued to rub the sleeves of his covering over his horse's coat, doing his best to dry the animal. "Thank ye, sir. I shall help ye in the cleaning of the stables come morning in payment for yer kindness. Ye are Arran, are ye not?"

Arran reached for a blanket draped over the doors of one of the stalls and moved to help Hew in his efforts. "Nay, that willna be necessary for ye to clean the stables. But, aye, I am Arran. Should I know ye, sir?"

Hew shook his head as they worked alongside each other, warming and drying the beast. "Nay, I doona expect that ye would remember me, but I believe ye know my sister, Mary. Is she still in service to yer family?"

The strapping lad next to him patted the horse gently on the backside before casting a rather surprised expression in his direction. "Nay, ye canna mean it? Ye're Mary's brother? Well, 'tis a pleasure to meet ye. And aye, we know Mary well, but I wouldna say she is in our service. This castle is more hers than my brother's."

Hew laughed. It seemed his sister had changed little over the years. "Aye, lad, that sounds verra much like she would have it. I dread the fuss she shall make over my arrival, but I feel I must make my presence here known to her. Where can I find her?"

Arran fidgeted uncomfortably. For a moment Hew worried that perhaps his sister was unwell, but the lad recovered quickly. "Well, it seems that she herself has gone on a bit of a journey, but doona worry about the weather, we know that she is quite safe and out of the storm. I shall let her explain to ye where it is she has gone once she returns."

Hew didn't understand what the lad meant, but he wasn't disappointed to learn that he would be able to rest before reuniting with his sister. "Ah, well, I'm certain she will be pleased to tell me all about it. She used to talk a great deal. I doona imagine that has changed."

Arran laughed and motioned for Hew to lead his horse into one of the empty stalls. "Nay, sir, she hasna changed. She's talked a lot for all the time that I've known her. Now, let us get yer horse settled, and ye shall follow me inside so that ye can have a room of yer own."

Hew stiffened and stopped moving forward. He would not be comfortable staying inside the castle. It was not where he belonged. He'd rather stay in the stables, with only the horses for company. "Nay, lad, I shall stay here with the horses. It would not be proper for me to accompany ye inside."

"Nay proper?" exclaimed Arran. "I willna be letting ye stay out here in this weather. If Mary learned I'd done so, she'd kill me herself, I'm certain."

Hew didn't wish to be impolite to his host, but staying in the stable was something he knew he must insist upon. He wouldn't sleep a wink in the presence of so many people. "I doona wish to offend ye, lad, but I simply canna stay in the castle. If ye willna allow me to remain out here, I'm afraid that Greggory and I will have to be on our way and take our chances with the snow."

Guilt filled Hew at the look of shock on Arran's face. If only the thought of company didn't paralyze him so.

"Nay, please doona leave in this storm. Mary would rather me allow ye to sleep in the stables, I'm certain. But perhaps, I can provide ye with something a little more comfortable than stable floors."

"Truly, lad, 'tis no trouble for me to stay here. I've slept in worse many times before."

Arran shook his head as he draped Hew's horse with coverings. "Just listen to me before ye say nay to it. We have a cottage not far from here. 'Tis empty. No one stays there, and ye are welcome to do so if ye wish. Ye can build ye a fire, and there is a proper bed. Please, sir, at least stay there."

Hew couldn't deny how pleasurable a warm fire and a soft bed sounded to him. As long as it was truly separate from the castle as the lad said, he thought he could find rest for the night there. "Aye, lad. I shall gladly stay in yer cottage. I'm sorry to be a bother to ye. I appreciate yer kindness."

Arran clasped him tightly on the shoulder. "Nay, sir, 'tis no trouble. I apologize for saying so, but ye're rather a strange fellow, are ye not?"

Hew laughed at the truthfulness in Arran's words as the young Conall showed him the way to the tiny cottage. "Aye, lad, that I am, verra strange indeed."

CHAPTER 6

Getting back to the seventeenth century was mildly tricky, but Mary and I managed. Because we brought with us two boxes of belongings and the precious vial I hoped would provide Bri with much relief once she went into labor, we were forced to sit on the floor of the spell room while we balanced the boxes in our laps. We chanted the words aloud together and reached over our boxes to link hands right before the spell began to work.

When we arrived back, we nursed our aching heads for a few short moments and then made our way up to the kitchen, where we heard Bri and her lookalike sister-in-law, Blaire, working together.

"We're back! What are you two girlies up to?" I set the box I carried down just past the doorway and went to give both of the girls a quick hug. I lingered an extra second with Bri, pressing my hands against her stomach to see if my grandbaby would give me a quick kick. For the moment, it seemed the infant slept soundly.

"We're trying to cook," said Blaire, in answer to my question. "But it isn't going so well. Eoin and Arran will be thrilled that yer home, Mary. They're convinced that if they have to go another day with us as cooks, they shall starve to death."

Bri winked at Mary and then bobbed her head in the direction of the box. "What did you get?"

I grabbed her hand and anxiously dragged her over so I could reveal all of the precious goodies we'd brought. "Morna knew what I wanted. She gathered up our ornament box. Isn't it wonderful?"

Bri moved to her knees instantly, her belly getting in the way, but I knew nothing would keep her from rummaging through the boxes. Each item was as special to her as it was to me. "Oh, Mom. You're joking! This is amazing, truly."

"Yes, it is, dear. She gathered a few other items for us, as well, but I'm going to wait until later to show those to you. It can just be a surprise for everyone." I placed my hand on her shoulder as I squatted down next to her. Then we lifted each tiny memory out of the box.

Blaire walked across the room to stand next to us. "The storm has slowed a bit. 'Tis still impossible to go too far from the main building, but not much is falling right now. Mayhap we should all go out together and find a tree to cut down for the decorations."

Bri leapt to her feet with more energy than I'd seen her exert in the last two months. "Yes, that's a perfect idea. I'll get Eoin. Blaire, you find Arran. Mom and Mary, go get Kip and meet us out back. Stat!"

She scurried off quickly, Blaire following suit. Mary and I laughed together, walking out of the kitchen so we could prepare for our outing.

*B*oth girls had apparently already decided that we would go tree hunting today if we returned from Morna's in time. The gathering of everyone went entirely too smoothly, as if they all waited on pins and needles for us to get home. The excitement of Christmas was starting to move through our merry little group.

The snow was beautiful, covering every inch of the castle grounds. I found myself wishing more than once that I'd enlisted Morna to cast us all a pair of sturdy snow boots to bring back. But we were all having such a wonderful time, none of us thought much about our ice-cold toes.

It took us some time before we found a tree that everyone agreed upon. We'd decided against many with the perfect shape that had proven far too large. And then some of perfect size had not been the right shape. Eventually, the perfect tree stood before us. While Eoin, Arran, and Mary's husband, Kip, worked at chopping it down, all of us girls huddled together, watching.

The landscape remained silent, save for the crack against the wood as the men took their turns driving the ax into its base. For a moment, I thought I'd imagined a soft whining sound coming from somewhere behind me, but as I listened I felt certain that I had not.

An animal, of that much I was sure, and a young one at that, made the noise. I couldn't tell what kind of creature it might be. My heart squeezed uncomfortably at the thought of anything so tiny and helpless being trapped out here in the snow.

Afraid that too many people approaching would cause it fear, I slowly crept away from the group and went off in search of the soft whine.

Hew stepped out in front of the small cottage, frowning as he looked out over the snow-drenched landscape. He'd hoped very much that he would be able to leave today, but it would be impossible. Even though snow no longer fell, he feared his horse might break a leg if he forced him to trudge through snow so deep.

He threw his arms up above him, stretching and groaning at his frustration. In response to the noises he made, something whined not far from him. Compassion compelled him to go in search of the creature.

Turning, he draped himself in thick coverings, the chill from his ride yesterday still set deep within his bones. Grunting, he took off in the direction of the noise. He stepped only a few feet away from the cottage when he caught sight of the dark, whimpering ball of fur at the base of the tree.

Hew bent, gently picking up the puppy, cradling it as it shivered uncontrollably in his large hands. He wrapped the pup up in his own furs, rubbing his hands back and forth over the small creature to warm it. It was a miracle the pup still lived, for it must have spent the previous night out in the storm.

Waiting for the puppy to stop trembling, Hew held it closely to his chest. When he felt its warm tongue start to lap at the inside of his fingers, he knew the pup was only cold, not injured. He uncovered the tiny animal, smiling as he took in its handsome features.

Hew raised him to check the gender and, finding him a boy, set him back into the cradle of his hand. The dog was fluffy with thick hair that made him look much bigger than he seemed. Its coat was dark on back, with a beautiful mixture of gray, brown and black spots covering his chest and feet. Warm brown eyes oozed kindness, and above them, small patches of light brown hair stood out, giving the illusion of brows.

"Why, ye are a handsome pup, are ye not?" He pulled the creature in close to him once more, reaching down to pick the clumps of icy snow from between the pup's paws. He stilled when another small whine caught his attention. "Ach, it seems that ye have another wee friend close by. Let's go find him together."

It had not taken me long to find the source of the noise. If not for the weak bark that the creature let out as I approached him, I would have probably stepped right on top of him, as the white of his fur matched the snow.

The puppy lay hidden close to the Conall's small cottage, with only his black nose and mouth sticking up out of the drift. I gasped when I saw him, quickly reaching down to snatch him out of his icy home, brushing the snow off of him with my bare hands. "Oh, you poor thing!"

The creature responded with another small bark. Once he was free of the snow, I lifted him, examining his coloring. His hair was straight but full—beautiful, but he was the kind of dog I was sure would shed easily. White fur covered most of his body, but his backside was black. With the exception of his white mouth and snout, each side of his face and both ears were black, too.

I'd expected the creature to squirm in my grasp but, once he became warm, he collapsed, relaxing completely, his small legs dangling on each side of my arm. I grinned as I pulled him in close. I hoped very much that Eoin would not object to having a dog in the castle because the pup would come with me, regardless.

A voice behind me caused me to jump, jerking my arm so that the puppy came awake, yipping in displeasure.

"Ah, I thought I heard another one making noise. Seems our two little friends must be brothers, aye?"

I turned around to face the most handsome man I had ever seen.

CHAPTER 7

"Oh my, you scared me. Hello there." I lifted my knees high as I moved closer to him. I didn't miss the strange expression that crossed his face when he heard me speak; everyone in this time had a similar reaction to my accent and twenty-first century way of expressing myself.

"'Ello to ye too, lass. I apologize for frightening ye. 'Twas not my intention. I heard this wee lad and found him not far from the one ye hold in yer hands. I still heard whining so I knew there must be another close by." He pointed to the black squirmy ball he held. His pup was far less content than the one cradled like broccoli in my arms.

Once close to the man, I extended my hand to touch the wiggly pup he held. The dog's fur felt soft like baby hair. As I rubbed him, the man reached his hand across to pet the pup I held.

"They are both fine looking pups, are they not?"

I nodded, and we simultaneously pulled our hands back to our sides. "Yes, beautiful dogs. Look at the markings above their eyes. They look quite different, but they must be out of the same litter."

"Aye, lass, I believe ye are right. They are the same size and age. Forgive me, miss. My manners are not what they should be. My name is Hew. To whom do I find myself speaking?"

I reached out to shake his hand. My stomach fluttered as he grabbed my fingertips and briefly touched them to his lips. I was far too old to have such a reaction to a man, but God he was a beautiful being. "Um…" I faltered and blushed, totally out of character from my normally over-confident, over-flirty self. "Um…Adelle. My name is Adelle."

I guessed he was only a few years older than me, if not the same age. Thick, dark, wavy curls, only lightly sprinkled with salt, covered his head. He kept it cropped short, unlike many men of this time who wore theirs longer. I preferred his. I didn't see the appeal in being with a man who had more hair on his head than I do.

Tall and broad shouldered, every inch of Hew was covered in clothing, but I had a feeling he would not be soft beneath the layers, like so many men from my time were by the time they reached my age. He worked hard; that was evident from the tone of his skin and the light crease of wrinkles across his brow. A light shadow of a beard only added to the manliness he exuded.

His awkward stance hinted at shyness. Now that we'd introduced ourselves to one another, he seemed uncertain of how to continue the conversation.

I had to shake my head to recover, yanking my stare away from the deep green abysses of his eyes. "Um…are you from around here? Do you live in the village?"

The puppy Hew held had stopped squirming and had fallen asleep in his arms. Bending his head to look at it, he said, "Nay, lass. I doona live anywhere near here. I'm on my way elsewhere but had to stop here due to the storm. I am staying in this cottage here." He pointed behind him. "The Conalls were kind enough to grant me refuge from the snow. My sister lives with them and works in the castle."

Only one woman worked for the Conalls, and other than myself, only one woman that wasn't a Conall actually lived in the castle. Mary was both. But there was no possible way the god that stood before me could be the brother Mary had been talking about. "You wouldn't be speaking of Mary, would you? Your sister is someone else, yes?"

Hew's eyes sparkled a brilliant green, creating another flurry of flutters in my stomach. "Aye, lass, 'tis Mary that I speak of. Do ye know her?"

Stunned, I stared at Mary's brother. I had based my mental image of him on her appearance, envisioning a short, round, aging bald man who talked loudly. This man was none of those things. His voice was deep, but he spoke quietly and said nothing more than required by the conversation. "Yes, I know Mary quite well. She's just around the corner here, along with everyone else from the castle. We've been cutting down a tree for Christmas. Does she know that you're here? Mary and I were away yesterday, we only just returned this morning."

He shook his head. "I doona know if she is aware of my presence yet, but I guess 'tis time that she is. Will ye lead the way to her for me, lass?"

"Of course." I turned and waved so he would follow me. I felt self-conscious with my back exposed to him. With every step, I damned myself for pinning my hair up into a hideous bun before we trekked out into the snow.

The group saw me first, and Mary immediately tore into me for stepping away from their company. "Adelle, what is the matter with ye? Why did ye run off without telling us where ye'd gone? Ye could have frozen to death…"

She paused when she caught sight of her brother, then moved

her short, stumpy legs faster than I'd ever have thought possible. Charging through the snow, she threw herself into his arms.

Hew let out a puff of air as she squeezed him, and then pushed her away as gently as he could. "Be careful, Mary. Ye shall squish the wee pup I hold in my arms."

Mary glanced briefly down at the sleeping dog but seemed unaffected by the adorable bundle. Bri and Blaire, on the other hand, immediately went to snatch the pups from each of our arms.

"What are ye doing here, Hew?" Mary exclaimed. "I havena seen ye in years. God, ye look good, brother!" Once Hew was free of the puppy, she threw her arms around him again.

"I was on my way to Mae's grave, but the storm caused me to seek shelter here," he explained. "I only arrived last evening."

The sadness I'd seen earlier in Mary briefly crossed her face again, and I wondered greatly about the identity of Mae. The pain showed only for a moment before Mary whirled away from her brother to face the crowd that had gathered, all of us watching curiously.

"I see," she said, her eyes narrowing. "And which one of ye knew he was here and dinna tell me the second I arrived this morning?"

Bri, Blaire, Eoin, and Kip all looked back and forth at each other, clearly in the dark, while Arran glanced sheepishly at the ground. "'Twas I, Mary," he said, after a moment of silence. "I apologize. I'm a fool. I got so caught up in the lasses' excitement over finding a tree that I forgot to tell ye."

I thought for a moment she would march through the snow and smack him, but her happiness at seeing her brother seemed to override her annoyance at not learning of his presence until now.

Mary tsked. "Shame on ye, Arran, but 'tis no matter now. Why doona the rest of ye go on back to the castle with the tree? I shall join ye shortly after I spend some time speaking with my brother, aye?"

"Aye, Mary," said Eoin, as he motioned for us all to head back. "Spend as much time as ye wish. I suppose we willna starve from only one more night of Bri and Blaire's cooking. Yer brother is welcome to dine with us, but if ye wish to spend some time alone together, I can bring ye food later this evening."

I was surprised when Hew responded to Eoin instantly. "I would be much obliged to ye if ye would allow us to dine in the cottage. I shall repay yer kindness in some way."

I couldn't blame him for not wanting to dine with everyone. We were a bit much to take. Still, his quick rejection seemed a little odd. He walked over to Blaire, who was holding his new puppy. After she handed it to him, he and Mary turned to make their way back to the cottage.

As we made our way the short distance back to the castle, both Bri and Blaire squeezed in tight on either side of me while I balanced my puppy in between my open palms. The girls leaned in close so that they could hear the other's whispers.

"Mom, holy cow, would you ever have thought Mary's brother would look like that?" Bri nudged my side playfully.

I smiled, laughing as I shook my head. I leaned into her, nudging her back. "No, not in a million years would I have expected that."

"Ye did find him a handsome lad, aye Adelle?" Blaire's voice was as quiet and excited as Bri's.

"Oh yes, very much so. He's quite striking. Why do you ask?" He must be married, of course. All the good ones were.

"He's a bit of a hermit from what Eoin and Arran told us," said Bri. "His wife died decades ago, and he lives all alone far away from anyone else. Seems a bit crazy to me, but Eoin seems to think he's just shy. Regardless, does it matter if he's crazy when he looks that good?"

The three of us laughed loudly, garnering questioning glances from the three men walking in front of us. Bri liked to think she was my polar opposite, but she was more like her Mama than she wanted to admit. "Well, it does matter a bit, yes, but I don't think he's crazy." We were approaching the castle. "Let's not gossip anymore now, the boys will give me a hard time." I lifted the puppy. "I'm going to find some food for this little one to eat."

Once inside, the girls dispersed. I carried the sleeping pup down into the kitchen while I thought over what I'd just learned about our new visitor. He was unmarried.

And I was not displeased to hear it.

CHAPTER 8

All was abuzz within the confines of Conall Castle the next day. It was decorating day. That, along with her brother's visit, lifted Mary's spirits as high as I'd ever seen them. As a result, everyone else in the castle couldn't help but be merry, as well.

I'd not expected us to put the tree in the castle's main entrance. I worried that the modern ornaments we planned to put on the tree might raise suspicions of other castle workers. I could not have been more surprised when I made my way down in the morning to find that Eoin, Arran, and Kip had placed the tree there.

"Wouldn't it be best if we set up the tree in the basement? I won't be able to hang the ornaments on it otherwise."

"Aye, ye will. Feel free to hang anything that ye wish from the tree. I willna have us hiding our celebrations. All who work within the castle know of Morna's legacy and her spells." Eoin walked up to me and bent to briefly kiss me on the cheek. "Good morning, Adelle."

I smiled, so very pleased that my daughter found such a

wonderful man. "Oh great, that's wonderful. It will look beautiful in the corner there, next to the grand fireplace."

"Aye, it will. Look." Eoin pointed to the staircase behind me. "Here come the other lassies. Let us eat and then we will begin the festivity of decorating."

Over breakfast, I couldn't help but notice Hew's absence from the table once again. I was fairly sure he hadn't left already. The snow still had not melted enough for travel, and there was little way for him to get food in the cottage without someone bringing it to him. I didn't understand why he seemed so set against joining us in the castle. Leaning closer to Mary, I asked, "Why won't your brother join us here to eat? He knows that he's welcome, doesn't he?"

Mary pulled one corner of her mouth to the side before casting sad eyes in my direction. "Aye, he knows it, but he insists on being alone."

"Why is that?" I looked down at my food so that my interest wouldn't seem too eager.

"He's painfully shy. He's spent so much time alone, I'm afraid he doesna know how to be around other people anymore."

That was a hard concept for me to grasp. I loved spending every second in the company of others. It was unhealthy for someone to live in such a way. It might be one thing for a person to spend time alone by their own choice, but another to feel that they were prevented from joining others due to shyness. "Well, the only way to become less shy is through practice. Will you see him this morning?"

Mary nodded. "Aye, I shall bring him something to eat as soon as we finish here and before we begin decorating."

"Ask him to join us and help in the decorations. It's going to be a lot of fun. Insist on it, Mary. You can be very persuasive."

Mary chuckled but shook her head. "That may be true with many people, Adelle, but nay with my brother. I can insist until the stars have risen, and it will not persuade him to do something he doesna wish to do."

I frowned. I didn't like the thought of Hew all alone in the cottage while the rest of us spent a joyous day decorating. "Well, will you at least ask him?"

Mary stood, covering a plate to take to her brother. "Aye, lass. I'll ask him."

Perhaps he'd been too short with his sister, Hew thought. It wasn't unreasonable for her to wish that he spend some time with her by joining in the Christmas festivities. He would make time to see her later when she was alone but his shyness would have done nothing but dampen the spirits of everyone else.

Hew no longer knew how to feel comfortable in front of one person, let alone an entire family of people who evidently were quite close to one another. He'd managed well enough when he'd bumped into Adelle the day he'd found the pup now sleeping at his feet, but that was an unusual occurrence. They'd had the discovery of the pups in common, which had given him something to talk to her about. Hew decided he would be certain to make an effort to spend a little more time with his sister before he left.

He reached down to rub on the sleeping pup, thinking back on the strangest thing his sister had told him. She'd said more than once that Adelle had insisted that he come to the castle and help them with the decorations. Why would the lass desire such a thing?

She must feel sorry for him. Any other possibility seemed too unrealistic for him to consider. There'd only been one woman to fancy him in his whole life. It wouldn't make sense for another lass to decide to do so now.

Would it?

CHAPTER 9

I waited until all of the men started trimming the tree, working it into the perfect shape, before sneaking away to grab the surprise I had in store for all of them.

Mary's trip to see her brother had been quick. When she arrived back at the castle without Hew, I knew he had rejected her invitation to join us. I couldn't help the small pang of sadness that lodged itself in my chest, but I did my best to dismiss it. I hardly knew the man, after all. What did I care if he chose to be such a fuddy duddy?

Blaire had already helped Bri carry the large box of ornaments upstairs, so while the men shaved away at the tree and the girls marveled at each ornament as they pulled them out of the box, I went down to the basement once more.

Opening the box, I pulled out the large boom box, flipping it over so that I could install a fresh set of batteries. Placing the CD player under one arm and a stack of CDs under the other, I made my way upstairs.

Once I got into the great room, I walked with my back toward everyone so as to shield the contents in my arms. Then I set the player discreetly next to the fire, hidden away behind a large chair. I thought it best to select a classical Christmas mix first. I was afraid anything too modern would frighten the bejeezus out of Arran and Kip, both of whom had never made a trip through time.

I started the music with the volume turned low. It played just loud enough to cause everyone in the room to glance around, as if they were imagining the sounds in their heads. Slowly, I increased the intensity until Kip threw both his hands to his ears and looked up to the ceiling in horror.

"What in the name o' God is that? I've told all of ye, I doona like the magic that seems to go on in this place. Make it stop."

Mary laughed and walked over to grab her husband's wrists. Prying his hands away from his head, she said, "Doona be such a fool, Kip. 'Tis not magic, only a music maker we brought back from our journey. Do ye not think it sounds lovely?"

When Kip didn't answer, Arran said, "I've never heard such beautiful noise in my life. Leave it be, 'tis magical."

Eventually, Kip surrendered and joined in with the humming and singing as we spent the day turning Conall Castle into a Christmas wonderland. The tree didn't take all that long, and after it was complete, Mary led us girls downstairs to make garland and wreaths to hang up around the castle.

It was hard work, twisting the leaves and branches into arrangements that pleased the eye. Mary, Blaire, and Bri took to it quite well, though. All of my projects, however, were undisputed disasters.

I'd not been a crafty woman in the twenty-first century, where craft stores on almost every other corner sold glues and tools to help with projects. Without such conveniences, I found even trying to attempt the endeavor to be pure misery.

After three failed wreaths and a string of garland only the

Grinch would appreciate, I was taken off craft duty and given the measly task of taking the mistletoe that Bri had created and hanging it above the dining hall entryway.

Mary thought the tradition of mistletoe to be a brilliant idea. "Ye mean that if I can somehow trick Kip into standing beneath the doorway with me, he will be forced to kiss me? Why, I shall stand there all day and wait for him to pass through! I doona believe the old bugger will even remember what part of yer body that ye use to kiss, 'tis been so long since he's done so."

I laughed, but as I did so, Mary's brother crossed my mind. If his life was anything like what Bri and Blaire had described, I imagined that it had been quite some time since Hew had been kissed, as well. For some reason, I wished to be the person to change that for him. "Mary, would you mind if I took Hew some food to eat after the evening meal?"

She clucked her tongue at me knowingly. "Ach, I knew there was a reason ye wished me to ask Hew to help with the decorations. Ye have taken a liking to him then, have ye?'

I reddened—something that seemed to be happening much more frequently than normal. I didn't like it one bit. "Well, what if I have?"

Mary laughed and looked down, concentrating on the bunch of stems in her hand. "Nothing, dear. It has been far too long since Hew has shared his company with another. Please, I would love for ye to take him his food. I doona like getting out in the snow anyway."

"Will he be angry, do you think? I don't want to upset him. I just thought perhaps I could bring some of the decorations that we didn't use, and I could leave them for him to set up at the cottage. It would give him something to do. With the snow still piled up, I don't think he will be leaving us anytime soon."

"Right ye are, lass, and he willna be angry at all. He's a kind man, although I'll admit that he is slow to warm. But once ye reach the man behind his shyness, the man he really is, why..." She paused, smiling down at her wreath. "Hew is a man worth getting to know."

CHAPTER 10

The cottage stood silent in front of Arran and me. I feared Hew had already gone to sleep for the evening. But when the puppy I cradled underneath my arm let out a high-pitched yelp, the door to the cottage flew open.

"Ach, evening, Adelle. Evening, Arran. I thought there was a third pup who had found his way out of the snow, but I see 'tis only yer little fellow, Adelle."

"Ah, yes." I paused and waved Arran away. Earlier, we'd cut down a small tree, and Arran had dragged it to the cottage, as well as helping me carry the food and decorations, which we'd set beside the door. "Thank you, Arran. I'll make it up to you somehow."

"Good night," Arran told us. "There is no need to make anything up to me, Adelle. Ye are quite welcome." He turned and started off, calling back to me over his shoulder, "Be careful on yer way back to the castle." Then he disappeared into the darkness, leaving Hew and me alone.

I silently thanked Arran for following my instructions to leave as soon as he dropped off all of the items. I wanted a chance to be alone with the quiet, strange man, and I didn't want to take the chance that Hew might ask Arran to stick around.

Not that I should've been concerned. With the look of surprise on Hew's face, I wondered if I would even be invited inside. I lifted up the basket of food I held in my left hand as I set my pup down on the ground. He immediately ran inside the cottage to join his brother. "Um…Mary was busy so I told her I would bring you something to eat. I hope you don't mind. Also . . ." I pointed to the items behind me, " . . . I brought some decorations. We had some left over from today, and I thought it would give you something to do, ya know, if you wanted to decorate the cottage for Christmas."

He scrunched his brows together. I couldn't tell if he was confused or disgusted. I'd not given much thought to the fact that he was a man and probably didn't give two flips about beautifying anything. I'd simply been trying to spread the cheer.

"I…you don't have to take the decorations. I can come back with Arran in the morning and get them," I stammered. "But at least take the food. I'll just head back to the castle now." I squatted awkwardly, whistling to my pup to come, but to no avail. The two brothers wrestled playfully on the floor with no intention of ending their little games anytime soon.

Hew surprised me by reaching out to put his hand on my shoulder. "Nay, lass, I shall enjoy the decorations. Please, come inside."

He stepped aside to usher me in, and I immediately complied, running my hands up and down my arms to warm myself.

"Come sit by the fire while I set the table," Hew instructed. "Surely ye are in no hurry to return to the castle. Why doona ye stay and eat with me? I'm sorry if I gave ye the feeling I wished for ye to leave. 'Twas simply that I was surprised by yer presence."

"Oh." I wanted to smack myself square in the forehead at my

inability to speak like a grown woman in front of him. My behavior was absolutely ridiculous. No man, not even Bri's father, had the ability to render me speechless so completely.

"Did ye already eat, lass? If so, I shall wait until after ye have gone. Perhaps ye can at least warm yerself by the fire for a little while, aye?"

For someone so shy, he tried to be talkative. And I rewarded his efforts by appearing far less friendly than I actually was. I needed to get a grip! I loved to talk and, by golly, I intended to do so. I set my mind to acting human again before I opened my mouth. "No. I haven't eaten."

He stood and moved to the small table, laying out the spread I'd brought for him. "Come and join me, lass."

We ate quietly. I searched my mind for ideas of what I could speak to him about, but came up short. I knew that Hew sensed my hesitation, as sometimes I would utter a syllable, only to stop before forming a complete word. He took pity on me by speaking himself.

"I apologize for the way I behaved when I opened the door. I am verra much accustomed to being all alone. Although I am a visitor here, visitors of my own are verra unexpected. Might I tell ye something?"

I nodded. "Of course."

"It occurred to me that perhaps ye keep stopping yerself from talking to me because ye are worried that I might notice the odd way in which ye speak."

That had nothing to do with it, but I didn't want to object when he had obviously put so much thought into my silence. Instead, I remained quiet and waited for him to continue.

"I confess that I did take note of it when I first met ye. But then Mary told me yer story about where and when ye came from and I understood. So doona worry, lass, I willna judge the way ye speak. I'm not so good at speaking with others myself."

Surprised by his words, I smiled. Mary hadn't lied. Her brother was a kind man. "How is it that you seem to have so easily believed what Mary told you? It is hard for even those of us who have experienced Morna's magic to accept it."

"Ach, ye have found yer voice. I am glad for it." Hew smiled slightly.

If I'd been standing, I expect my knees would have grown weak at the beauty of that smile.

"I knew Morna when I was a child, and I grew up hearing stories of her powers," Hew explained. "I know my sister well enough to know that she wouldna lie to me about such a matter. Besides, life is such that many things happen that we canna explain. It must have been quite a change for ye to come here, aye?"

Our food was now gone, and I knew I would be expected to take my leave soon. "Yes, it was, but one I welcomed. With my daughter being here, there's nowhere else I'd rather be. I love it here very much." I stood, pushing my chair in before walking to the door. "Why don't I help you carry the rest of these things in? Then I'll leave you be for the evening."

The same unreadable look that had crossed his face earlier resurfaced, and I was afraid I'd somehow upset him. He cast his palm out in the direction of the empty room. "Are ye not going to stay and help me? It seems ye have brought enough trinkets to decorate an entire village, and I havena celebrated the holiday since I was a small child. I'm afraid I shallna know what to do with all of it on my own."

I beamed and stepped out into the darkness so he wouldn't see my reddened face. "Yes, I would love to."

For someone that didn't like the company of others, he seemed to be in no hurry to rid himself of mine.

---

*H*ew thought the lass must still carry Morna's magic with her for her to have such an effect on him. He'd been surprised by her slim presence at the door. And pleased when she'd quickly sent Arran away, her blonde hair blowing wildly in the breeze. She wanted to be alone with him. While Hew wasn't sure why, the thought made something deep within him warm for the first time in ages.

At first, Adelle had seemed even more nervous than he. That fact somehow helped to calm his nerves in the beauty's presence. In fact, he felt very much himself with her and talked as freely as he did with anyone.

The lass's shyness had not lasted long. After he'd asked her to stay and help him with the decorations, she'd talked with him at length, telling him grand stories of all that had happened at Conall Castle within the last months. For the first time, Hew found himself wishing he had not stayed away from his homeland for so long.

When all that Adelle had brought him was set up just as the lass would have it, he walked her back to the castle, his heart more sad than he would allow himself to admit that their evening together had come to an end.

"Thank you for allowing me to interrupt your evening," she said. "I hope I wasn't too much of a bother."

The lass was mad if she was unable to see how much he had enjoyed her company. Perhaps his feelings dinna show clearly on his face. He had kept them locked away deep inside himself for a verra long time, after all.

He stared directly into her green eyes now, eyes so vibrant

and alive that he couldn't help but realize how little he'd allowed himself to truly live for far too many years. She was the most beautiful woman he had ever seen, her pale face pink from standing out in the cold. He wanted to do nothing more than warm it with the touch of his lips.

"Nay, lass, ye were not a bother at all. I had a wonderful time," Hew said quietly.

Mustering all the courage he had left in him for the evening, he quickly leaned in to kiss her on her cheek. Turning before he could see her reaction, he marched back into the darkness, his heart beating faster than it had in decades.

CHAPTER 11

Carrying my pup, I left my bedchamber early the next morning to join everyone in the dining hall for breakfast. Still high on the endorphins Hew's lips had stirred in me the night before, I reminded myself that it had only been a kiss on the cheek, but the reminder did nothing to push the giddy flurries away. What would I have done if he'd given me a proper kiss?

I found myself imagining such a kiss, then pushed the vision from my mind. I was going to be a grandmother for goodness' sake. I had no business acting like a silly schoolgirl with a crush.

But honestly, who was I kidding? Even though I was a grandmother-to-be in my fifties, I'd always been young on the inside, immature some would say, and I didn't have hope that a grandchild would change that about me any time soon. I'd given up acting my age—whatever that meant—long ago.

I walked into the dining hall and felt my eyes widen in surprise. Hew sat at the table along with everyone else. Doing my best to hide my shock, I sat at my usual place, setting my puppy on the floor at my feet. Then I turned to listen to Eoin, who was addressing the table.

"Are ye finished with yer meal, lads? If so, let us be on our way. I'm not so inclined to leave Bri's side, but she was verra insistent that we make this trip."

Bri nodded and waved him off, patting her stomach with her other hand. "Yes, I was. Be gone, all of you, and have a wonderful time. The baby seems content where it is. I'm certain it will be days until the birth."

"Where are you going?" I asked. I'd obviously missed the front of this conversation. Regardless, I was not willing to be left out of the loop.

"Since Christmas Eve is only days away, the men are leaving us for a few days to go on a hunt," Bri responded from across the table. "Hew has agreed to stay with us until after the holiday. He's going to help them on the hunt. Mary says he is a fine shot with an arrow."

I glanced at Hew, then quickly away. "Wonderful. Are you boys certain you trust us to have free run of the castle while you're away?"

Eoin laughed as the other men rose from their places at the table. "Oh, Adelle. Ye all have free run as it is, do ye not?"

I had nothing to say to that. He was right. We most certainly all did exactly as we wished. Headstrong women filled Conall Castle.

As the men prepared to leave, Hew walked around the table to stand at my side. He carried his puppy, which had been hidden underneath the table at his feet, just like mine.

"Will ye watch over him for me while I am away, lass?" My pup had ventured out from beneath the table and Hew set his beside it. They instantly began gnawing at each other's faces playfully. "They seem quite attached to one another."

I grinned, nodding emphatically, pleased and surprised that he'd decided to join the men on their hunt. "Of course. I'll take excellent care of him."

"Aye, I'm sure ye will, lass."

He turned and left without bidding farewell to anyone else in the room, even Mary, and I could almost see the steam coming from her ears.

Mary waited all of five seconds after the men left the dining hall to tear into me. "Did ye lead my brother to believe that ye care for him more than ye do, Adelle? Are ye not bothered that he will be hurt by yer pretense? Hew is not like other men who are amused by a woman's teasing."

My mouth fell open in response to her attack. "What? Are you mad? Of course I didn't pretend any such thing! I didn't do anything save talk his ear off. He was very kind to put up with me. I enjoyed his company very much."

Mary's expression changed from one of anger to sheer surprise. "So ye swear to me then, ye are not simply amusing yerself by teasing him into thinking the likes of ye would enjoy being with such a shy man? What did the two of ye talk about? My brother hardly speaks two words in a week's time."

Whatever anger that had faded from Mary had moved into me. "Mary, if I weren't afraid you would knock me flat on the floor, I'd be half tempted to throttle you right now. It is absolutely none of your business what your brother and I talked about. And you insult me by thinking I'd toy with his feelings."

"Since he willna talk, did ye fill the time by trying to kiss him, then?"

Bri and Blaire glanced nervously at one another, and I could tell they wondered if they should stand in between us to keep us from attempting to strangle one another. Both of us needed to calm down.

"No, I did no such thing, Mary."

"Oh." Mary stood and walked around the room, as if trying to accept my words as truth.

"Oh, is right. You should feel mighty ashamed of yourself for assuming such a thing." I leaned back in my chair, crossing my arms to show my frustration.

Bri blinked at me. "Mom, in Mary's defense, Hew is her brother. He has been alone for a long time and he's a gentle and sensitive man. She's only looking out for his best interests, and it's not as if what she accused you of doing would be completely out of character for you, besides."

I shot my daughter a look that must have been frightening for she sank down into her chair and didn't say another word as we all waited for Mary to speak again.

Eventually, she exhaled exaggeratedly and moved to resume her seat at the table. "Well, if the two of ye dinna even kiss, my brother must fancy the oddest of women, because he's mighty taken with ye."

"Why do you say that?" My face warmed, and I reached up to fan myself. At least at this age, I could use hormones as an excuse.

"I all but begged him to join us as ye bid me to yesterday, and he would not come. He spends one evening in yer company, and he shows up at the castle this morning without being asked. He's always welcome o'course, but 'tis shocking behavior from him, Adelle. He even suggested the hunt. He went to Eoin early this morning and told him that he thought he'd found some great places for hunting on his way here."

"Is that so?" I looked down at myself. If only there was air conditioning in this century.

Bri smiled and pointed at my face. "Mom, you're blushing. You like him, don't you?"

My daughter was skating on thin ice this morning. "Yes, I do, but I am not blushing. I'm far too old to blush. It's just very warm in here, is all. I think I'm having a hot flash."

"Nay, Adelle," said Blaire, ganging up on me along with Bri. "'Tis not warm in here at all. I doona believe ye are having a flash of warmth. I think Bri is right, ye're blushing."

"Why don't the two of you just bugger off?" I stood, determined to go find some cold water to splash on my face. At the doorway, I paused and looked back at the threesome. "Oh, Mary," I said, my old spunk returning. "I didn't lie when I said that I didn't kiss your brother." Smiling, I added, "*Hew* kissed *me*."

CHAPTER 12

The men stayed close to the castle, finding shelter for themselves and their horses in the village. The hunt had done them all good. Hew was accustomed to spending his days working hard on his land. He didn't like being cooped up in the confines of the small cottage each day.

He'd wanted to learn more about Adelle from his hosts while away, but had hoped to keep his growing feelings for her a secret. He'd been completely unsuccessful. It seemed all of the men had assumed that his sudden eagerness to join in the castle activities had something to do with her.

As they made their way to the rooms they'd rented at the inn for the evening, Arran nudged him in the ribs as if they'd known each other forever. "Did ye enjoy Adelle's visit last night? Ye must have, for I had no luck convincing ye to step inside the castle walls, while she had no problem doing so at all."

Hew couldn't lie to him. Just the thought of Adelle made something deep within his chest hum with an excitement he'd thought himself no longer capable of feeling. "Aye, lad. I verra much enjoyed the time we spent together."

"And ye find her a bonny-looking lass, do ye not?"

The lad was forward, but Hew expected it was how he was with everyone. Arran didn't seem the kind of man to mince words, no matter with whom he conversed. "Aye, she's as beautiful a lass as I have ever seen. Do ye know her well, Arran?"

"Aye. I've spent much of the last year with her. She's wonderful, although a bit more forthright with her words than most lasses. I wouldna have her any other way, though. Mary, Blaire, and Bri are much the same, so perhaps that is why I doona mind her so much. I find fiery lasses to be the best company."

"Nay, I doona mind it, either. My wife was verra much like that. She always said whatever came to her mind. 'Twas a treasure to be with such a woman. I never had to guess what she was thinking." Hew smiled, slightly surprised at himself. It was the first time he'd spoken of his wife that sadness hadn't crept into his heart.

"Well, ye never have to wonder what Adelle is thinking, 'tis certain," said Arran with a chuckle. "Ye shall be joining us for the meal on Christmas Eve, aye? It would disappoint her if ye dinna, and I can tell by the sparkle in yer eye when ye speak of her that ye doona wish to do that."

The last thing Hew wanted to do was upset Adelle in any way. Slowly but surely, he found himself wanting to do nothing less than please her. "Aye, lad, I'll be there. Ye are right, I doona wish to disappoint her at all."

---

*T*he men returned to the castle midday on Christmas Eve. The prizes of the hunt were such that I was immediately forced to join Mary in the kitchen so that we could get started preparing the meat. Bri and Blaire somehow evaded the kitchen. I suspected they were both spending private moments with their husbands, whom they'd not seen for an entire three days.

It seemed a bit ridiculous to me that such a short period of separation seemed to cause them both such distress. Even so, I was a little envious of the relationships they had found. I'd never had that sort of bond with Bri's father. We both celebrated at the absence of the other. Even after our divorce, I'd never dated anyone long enough to allow my feelings to become very strong.

By the time all of the food was prepared, everyone but Mary and I waited anxiously in the dining hall, ready to devour the feast that was about to be placed before them. I'd just stepped into the room when I tripped on the bottom of my dress, causing me to lunge forward.

I was certain I would land on the floor, spilling the precious bread basket I held, but Hew's quick reflexes suddenly set me right. He'd jumped up to pull a piece of garland out of his curious puppy's mouth and had passed by me just in time to prevent my fall.

"Are ye all right, lass? Mary would kill ye if ye dropped the food."

"Yes, she most certainly would. Thank you." I looked up at him, instantly lost in the greenness of his eyes. He didn't let go of my forearms, and it took Arran's voice from the table to break the lock of our gazes.

"Look up," Arran said, pointing above our heads. "Ye have both found yerself beneath the mistletoe. Ye must kiss her, Hew. 'Tis bad luck if ye doona."

Our eyes met again. I was certain Hew wouldn't kiss me. It had seemed a major accomplishment for him to have kissed my cheek in private. Mistletoe or not, a public display of affection would be too much to ask of him.

He didn't glance away. Instead, leaning in so close that his lips were only a hair's width from mine, he whispered, "It seems that I must. I willna have bad luck following ye, lass."

His lips pressed warmly against mine, soft and shy. I melted into him, winding my fingers up into his hair as the butterflies in my stomach took flight, coursing through every inch of my body.

"Well, now ye have gone and ruined it," Mary said, her voice causing Hew to break the kiss and pull away from me. She pointed up at the mistletoe. "Now that Kip has seen what that is for, I shall never be able to trap him beneath it."

Hew laughed, but leaned in close to my ear after Mary passed by us, whispering so quietly that no one but I could hear him. "I intend to finish that kiss later, lass," he said, sending chills of delight up my spine.

I smiled, not caring about the eyes focused on us. "I surely hope so," I whispered back to him.

CHAPTER 13

Christmas morning was all that I'd hoped it would be. Presents, a beautiful tree, a warm fire, and lots of love and laughter filled the castle. Together, we lit the candle to place in the window, lighting the way for strangers—a New Year's tradition Mary shared with us. I'd heard of the custom through my archaeological studies, but it was a treat to be an active participant in the ritual.

When Bri opened the baby blanket, she cried big fish tears that soon had all of the women, even Mary, blubbering like babies. My grandbaby was due to arrive any day now, so I'd also wrapped up the vial Morna had sent along with me. Bri's reaction was just what I had expected.

"Oh, thank God! For weeks, I've been so terrified about the pain I would experience without medication." She placed both palms lovingly on her belly and laughed. "I'd about made up my mind that I was not going to let this child come out. If the medicine came from Morna, it's certain to help, don't you think?"

I suspected she might be getting her hopes up a little too high. While I was sure Morna's potion would help to take the edge off somewhat, I knew from my own experience that even with modern medicine, childbirth was seldom, if ever, a pain-free experience. I didn't imagine that's what she wanted to hear, though, so I simply smiled and nodded. "Yes, I'm sure it will help."

Hew had joined us but remained standoffish. I assumed he didn't want to make any of us feel guilty for not having gifts for him. I did, however, have something for him. It just wasn't quite ready yet, and I didn't want him to know about it until later. I would need to enlist Mary's help to finish it, as I'd done a fantastic job of thoroughly screwing it up.

I walked over to him, gently reaching out to touch his arm. "Merry Christmas."

He smiled and gently squeezed my hand. "Merry Christmas to ye, as well, lass. It has been many years since I have been able to witness such a wonderful celebration, but now I believe I shall take my leave and return to the cottage for awhile."

"Oh, please don't. We all enjoy having you here. Do you feel uncomfortable?"

"Nay, lass. I am surprised to say that I am verra comfortable with all of ye. 'Tis only that I have something I'd like to give ye but 'tis not quite finished. Would ye stop by the cottage in a little while?"

I smiled, but panic rushed through me. "Yes, of course I will." I wasn't going to accept a gift from him unless I had something to give him in return. That meant I didn't have much time to convince Mary to help me fix the disaster I had tried to sew together yesterday morning.

Hew smiled, squeezing my hand once more before he slipped away. As soon as I saw him gone, I crossed the room to yank Mary up from her chair.

"You have to come help me, quick. I tried to make Hew something, but I've messed it all up. Now he's going to give me a gift, so I need you to repair my disaster so I'll have a present to give him in return."

"Ach, I see how he is. He will give you a gift—a complete stranger until just a short time ago—but has nothing for his sister. Did I just hear ye say ye tried to sew something, Adelle?"

"Yes," I said, adding, "I know. It was a horrible idea."

Mary looked at me begrudgingly but stood. I knew she would be happy to help. "Aye, lass." She laughed heartily. "Ye are a fool, but I'm so happy this Christmas morning, I doona mind telling ye that I love ye dearly. Now, let's go fix the mess ye've made. My brother deserves a proper gift."

CHAPTER 14

Cradling the puppy close to my chest, I knocked on the door to the cottage with numb fingers, my red nose sniffling as I waited. It had started snowing again and the wind blew bitterly cold. Hew opened the door quickly, smiling wide.

"Come inside, lass. Ye and the pup both. 'Tis freezing outside."

A large fire burned from the hearth, making the room warm, almost toasty, inside. Hew wore less clothing than usual—long pants, a thin linen shirt that exposed the upper part of his chest. I swallowed hard at the sight of the dark hair peeking out just beneath his Adam's apple.

Once I stepped inside and lowered the pup to the floor, Hew pulled me into a warm embrace. I breathed in the masculine scent of him, my face pressed so closely to his chest I could feel the beat of his heart. "I'm sorry it took me so long to get here," I said softly. "I had to coax Mary to help me finish your gift. I made quite a mess of it on my own."

Moving away from me, he crossed the room to grab a small box that sat on the windowsill next to the tree. "Ye doona need to give me a gift, lass."

"Well, same goes for you, then. But, it seems that we both did anyway, so let's exchange them."

I didn't wait for him to give me mine before extending the two folded pieces of cloth I held in my hands. He took them, and after unfolding them, stared down at the odd pieces quizzically. "Thank ye, lass, but what exactly is it that I'm holding?"

I bent down and snatched up my puppy, which had been snuggling next to his brother near the fire. Reaching out, I took one of the cloth pieces from Hew and gently slipped it over the puppy's head, pushing each leg through the tiny holes.

He laughed loudly. "Did ye truly make a shirt for the pups? Is this a common thing where ye come from?"

I smiled. I knew he would find it silly, but there was no denying how precious both of them would look in their small, wool onesies. "Yes, I surely did. Not all that common, but a few crazy people like me do sometimes dress their dogs. You can't deny how cute they look."

He grinned, picking up the other pup and slipping my other small creation over the animal. "Nay, lass, I canna deny it. They shall be the bonniest, most ridiculous-looking pups anywhere. It seems that our gifts will complement each other."

"Oh, really? How?"

He placed the box inside my hands. "Open it and see, lass. I hope ye like them. It has been some time since I carved anything."

The box itself was exquisite, crafted by fine hands. I could only imagine how magnificent the contents inside would be. I lifted the top gently and took off the small piece of cloth covering the items. When I saw what lay beneath it, I had to choke back tears.

Two wooden ornaments lay nestled within, each perfectly carved into the shape of a dog—a puppy, to be exact. The ornaments dangled from two matching crimson ribbons. I glanced down at the pups snuggling on the floor at our feet, marveling at how closely the ornaments resembled the two creatures that had first brought Hew and I together.

I'd not had a gift so touching in many years. It wasn't the ornaments themselves, although they were certainly impressive. The attention and thought that had gone into such a gift touched me deeply. Hew had obviously listened to me the night we'd decorated the cottage together, and taken special note of my love for such objects.

"Do ye not like them, lass?" he asked, his voice startling me. "I'm not as good at crafting wood as I once was. I'm a bit out of practice."

"No." I reached out to grab him firmly by the hand. "They're amazing, Hew, truly. I love them. It's only that . . . I'm a little disappointed." I grinned flirtatiously at the concern in his expression.

"Disappointed, lass?"

"Yes, disappointed. I was hoping your gift to me would include finishing that kiss we started."

He laughed, ripping the box from my hands, tossing it onto the bed across the room, and pulling me tightly against him. "Aye, I'll finish it, lass, and then I'll begin another. And another."

This kiss held none of the shyness of the first one. Hew's lips moved confidently against my own as, with one hand pressed to my lower back, he brought me closer to him. The fingers of his other hand wound into my hair.

"Ach, lass," he said into my ear when he finally pulled away, the touch of his breath sending a cascade of shivers across my skin. "Doona tease me so again about being disappointed. If ye want me to kiss ye, all ye have to do is ask..."

I laughed at the tickling sensation his words spread down my neck and back. "I'm sorry. I didn't mean to tease you, Hew. Next time, I'll know."

"And when will this next time be, lass?"

"How about now?"

He cocked a brow. "What did I tell ye?"

I smiled and narrowed my eyes. "Kiss me," I said coyly.

He kissed me lightly at first. I kissed him back just as gently. We learned the feel of each other's arms, the texture of lips, the taste of one another. I felt lightheaded as his breath merged with mine, and I had the oddest feeling that despite the delicious newness of our relationship, he was familiar, someone I'd known deep down in my heart for a very long time. Someone I'd been waiting for, that I was supposed to meet.

If I didn't pull away and change the subject quickly, I was afraid I would allow this experience to go to a place I was not ready for yet. Not that it wouldn't be nice, but something in my mind screamed that this man needed to be different than the men I'd known in the past. He *was* different. Special. And I wanted our relationship to be different and special, as well.

Slowly, I stopped the kiss and pulled back. "I just thought of something."

His green eyes were hazy, nearly blurred with the pleasure that I was certain mirrored my own gaze. "Aye? What is that, lass?" he asked. "Do ye think perhaps ye could tell me later? With you in my arms, I can't think at all."

I laughed and tried to step away, but he held me close to him. "No, it's very important. We have yet to name our puppies. We found them together. I think we should name them together."

Hew remained quiet for a moment, then said, "Aye, lass, ye are quite right. We should do it together. And I know just what I wish to name the dark one."

I tilted my head to one side, studying him. "Really? What?"

"He's quite a masculine pup, do ye agree? His fur makes him look like an exotic beast. I think we should name him Tearlach. It means that he is a manly creature."

I smiled. I didn't think the puppy looked manly, only

adorable, but he was right. As the pup grew, the fluffy hair around his head would make him look like a lion. "It's the perfect name for him," I said.

"Ye should be the one to name the lighter one. 'Tis ye that found him."

I thought for a moment, but every name I came up with sounded too American. My pup needed a name as noble and Scottish as his brother's. "Do you see how his tail always sticks up? It looks like he is waving a flag. Is there a word for that?"

"Aye, lass, I see. What about Bratach? It holds much the same meaning."

"Bratach. I like it!" I stood on my tiptoes and kissed Hew's cheek. "I think it's perfect, and with that I will take my leave. You are too much of a temptation for me to stay a moment longer."

He laughed, a deep, grumbled sound that shook his whole chest and made my knees go weak.

"Temptation, lass? Nay, 'tis ye that are the temptation. I have been alone for a long time. Ye have awakened feelings within me I fear I am too old to handle."

"You are not old," I said indignantly. "You're the same as me, I'd imagine, and I am in no way old, which means neither are you." I moved to stand by the door.

"If you say so, lass. Will ye accompany me somewhere tomorrow afternoon?"

"Yes, I think I could manage that. Where?"

"'Tis a surprise, lass. I shall meet ye at the back of the castle come midday."

He opened the door to the cottage, taking my hand so he could walk me back to the castle, leaving me to wonder just what tomorrow held in store for me.

CHAPTER 15

Hew rose early the next morning to work on carving the large piece of wood left over from the ornaments he'd made for Adelle. He hoped to shape it into a sort of sled that he and Adelle could take on their outing this afternoon.

Just thinking about spending more time with her made his heart beat more quickly. He'd lived alone for too long. He realized now that he had convinced himself that a solitary life was the only way to honor the memory of his late wife. And so he'd remained wrapped in his memories of their brief time together. Memories that should have been a blessing instead of the trap he'd made them into. Adelle had changed all of that. Since meeting her, he felt released from his self-imposed prison, and more alive than he could ever recall feeling. He was slowly learning that choosing a solitary life had not honored his late wife; in fact, nothing could have been further from the truth.

Mae had not been a jealous woman. She knew she held his heart and lived her life with more light and love than any other lass he'd ever met. She would've wished more for him. She wouldn't have been pleased that he'd spent so many years all alone.

It saddened him that, for so long, he'd not realized the mistake he was making.

All he could do now was to try and move forward, living the rest of his life as Mae would've wished it. She would be very pleased to know that he'd found happiness once again. He could almost hear her whispering in his ear, pleading with him not to let Adelle slip out of his grasp.

He didn't intend to do any such thing, but he also knew it would be best that they spend their afternoon together out of doors. He was a man who'd gone too long without the company of a woman. He would only make his situation more difficult if he allowed himself to be alone with her for an extended period of time within four walls. Adelle was too special a woman to dishonor her, and he was not the sort of man to do so, anyway.

For this reason he worked, chipping away at the wood with as much force as he could muster, crafting it into the perfect seat for two. He must exert whatever physical activity he could to help keep his mind off of his need for her.

---

*E*ither Hew hadn't told Mary what he planned for us to do this afternoon, or she was simply determined not to reveal what she knew.

She and Bri insisted on grooming me for my outing with Hew, and they'd decided to dress me in the finest frock I owned. "Are you sure this is appropriate? I feel very overdressed," I said.

"It's always better to be overdressed than underdressed," my daughter quipped. "I believe you are the one that taught me that. Besides, we have no way of knowing, do we, since Mary refuses to reveal her brother's plans?"

As Bri continued to pick away at my hair, doing her best to pin it into place, Mary threw her hands up in exasperation. "I already told ye, I doona know what his plans are," she screamed. "I havena spoken to him about it. Ye are a couple of thick-headed lassies, the two of ye!"

She turned and left us, stomping her feet on the way out the door. Once she was gone, laughter burst out of us. "I should not have pestered her so. There. What do you think?" asked Bri.

She stepped away so that I could turn and look in the mirror. "Thank you," I said, eyeing my reflection. "My hair looks nice, but I feel ridiculous in this dress. I'd rather be in jeans and a nice blouse."

Bri laughed and bent down to squeeze me while placing her face up against my own. "I'm sure you would, but those days are over, I'm afraid. At least it's not expected that we shave our legs in this time."

"Thank God for small mercies." She was right. It would have been considered quite strange for us to do so in this time and that was fine with me. I always thought it a pain in the rear anyway.

"Are you nervous, Mom? You like Hew quite a lot, don't you?"

I stood, wishing I could shorten the dress a good eighteen inches just so I would be able to move more freely. "I do like him a lot, and I admit to being a little nervous. But every time I'm around him, whatever nerves I may have had before dissipate quickly." I averted my gaze, suddenly embarrassed. "I'm probably being foolish. Once the snow melts, he'll no longer want to stay here."

"I wouldn't be so sure, Mom. I think if he had reason to stay, he would. You may just end up being that reason."

I hoped she was right. The thought of him leaving filled me with sadness, but I would not worry about that now. Today, I was simply going to enjoy his company.

CHAPTER 16

Sneaky Mary had known exactly what activity Hew had planned for us. When he arrived at the back entrance of the castle carrying a sled, I caught sight of Mary hiding around a corner, cackling like a banshee.

"It is not the least bit funny, Mary! Now he will be forced to wait on me while I change. There's no way I'm going to get this dress sopping wet."

Mary stepped out from her place in the shadows, laughing as she waved her brother inside. "Oh, doona be such a grumpy bairn, Adelle. Hew, get yerself inside whilst the lassie changes."

Hew stomped his snow-covered feet off outside before following Mary's instruction, casting me an apologetic glance before reprimanding his sister. "'Twas not kind of ye, Mary." He turned to me. "But I willna say I'm not pleased to see ye in such a fine dress, lass. Ye look lovely."

Mary piped up once again, not giving me a chance to thank him for his kind words.

"Ach, if ye find her pleasing in that, I'm sure ye shall fall over when ye see what she will come down in next. I'm certain she will use yer idea of playing in the snow as the perfect excuse to don her horrific garb from her own time. I doona see what the lads seem to see in it, but every time Adelle, Bri, or Blaire decide to squeeze themselves into their modern clothes, all the lads, my own Kip included, can hardly keep their tongues inside their mouths. 'Tis truly pathetic."

Hew's brows pulled together quizzically, but he said nothing. I ignored her, as well, and turned to make my way back upstairs.

I was almost out of sight when Mary called out to me, "I'm right, aye? Ye are going in search of yer 'jeans?'"

I smiled at the anticipation of ripping this burdensome dress off and sliding into the comfy denim. I yelled over my shoulder back at her. "Yes, Mary. You are very right, indeed."

*M*ary had also been right about Hew's reaction to seeing a woman in such clothing. It was certainly a sight men in this time were unaccustomed to seeing. His mouth nearly fell open when I came back downstairs. Though entirely covered from head to toe, and bundled up for our snowy activities, I suddenly felt self-conscious under his gaze.

"Ach, lass, I doona know if ye should trust yerself with me when ye look as ye do. Do women commonly dress in such a manner where ye come from?"

I laughed and marched out into the snow ahead of him. "Yes, all the time. This is quite a conservative outfit, I assure you. Would you rather I put my dress back on?"

He caught up to me quickly, throwing his arms around me from behind and kissing me roughly on the cheek. "Nay, lass," he said, his facial hair tickling my ear. "I wouldna let ye go and change even if ye wished it. Come. I found a bonny hill near the cottage that shall be perfect for sledding."

I was both excited and surprised by his choice of activity. Hew was much more fun than he'd originally let on. Taking his hand in my own, we made our way to the snowy hill.

The lass meant to torture him. No other explanation made sense for her to have dressed the way she had. There was no hiding her shape in the trousers, and what a fine shape it was. Curvy in all the right places, as a woman should be.

Hew breathed in deeply through his nose, hoping the chill in the air would cool the fire that burned inside him. Thankful when they reached the hill, he promptly placed the sled down onto the snow and instructed Adelle to sit in the front so that he could join her on the back end.

Pushing off hard, they flew down the snowy landscape, both of them howling with delight as the cold wind rushed across their faces. When the sled finally reached the bottom of the hill, it stopped rather abruptly, uprooting both of them from their seats, sending them tumbling out into the snow.

They landed in a twisted pile. Adelle was on top of him, laughing so hard that the trembling of her chest shook his own.

"Are ye all right, lass?" Their fun would be spoiled quickly if his idea of going sledding had caused her harm.

She smiled brightly, bending to quickly kiss him on the tip of his nose. He found himself wondering how a lass could manage to keep her teeth so brilliantly white. They were stunning, just like every other part of her.

"Yes, I'm fine. Let's go again!"

She leapt off of him and was halfway up the hill before he could manage to roll over and climb his way out of the snow.

CHAPTER 17

"Wakey, wakey…"

Bri's voice lured me out of a deep sleep. I awoke to find Bri and Blaire sitting on either side of me, grinning in anticipation.

I rolled onto my stomach, shielding my face from the both of them, groaning as I spoke. "What do you want? Just leave me alone. I'll wake up sometime tomorrow."

Bri stuck her hand into my hair, mussing it about so that I would turn over onto my back. "You missed breakfast. So did Hew. Mary's not pleased with either one of you, and she said that you will just have to wait until evening to eat because she wasn't going to warm anything for you once you woke up."

I obliged her and rolled over, sitting myself up so that I was eye level with both of them. Endlessly hungry, I could out eat almost any man. No way would I wait until evening to eat. "That's not happening. I am more than capable of feeding myself. Mary is not going to dictate when and what I eat."

Bri looked over at Blaire who laughed knowingly. "What did I tell you, Blaire? I knew she would say something like that."

"Hicumm…excuse me," I said, clearing my throat to gain

control of their attention again. "I'm right here, you know. Now, what are the two of you doing in here?"

I knew well enough why they'd come, but Blaire obliged me by answering my question. "Why do ye think we have come? We wish to hear all about yer afternoon yesterday."

Thinking back on the day, I couldn't help but grin. It had been a wonderful afternoon and ages since I'd laughed so hard. My stomach would be sore for a week from the effort of it. I ached from head to toe, bruised from the many spills I'd taken into the snow, but every tight muscle was worth it. "Well, we honestly didn't do much of anything except sled down the giant hill near the cottage about a thousand times."

Bri smiled as she held on to her swollen belly. "Did you have a good time?"

"Aye, o'course she did. She canna keep from grinning." Blaire winked at me, but her expression quickly shifted to concern. "But ye seem to have had a wee bit too much fun, Adelle. Ye are mighty red."

I reached up and touched my face, flinching at the pain. My cheeks felt quite swollen. There was little in the way of sunscreen in this time, and I'd not thought to cover my face, even after I learned we were to spend the day sledding. "I'll have to see if Mary has any herbal salve I can put on this to calm it down a bit. How bad do I look?"

"Completely terrible," said my daughter.

My eyes widened in surprise. With each passing day Bri grew more uncomfortable in her pregnancy, and she was becoming increasingly blunt with her words. "Ouch. Thanks, Bri, but I suppose it's my own fault. I really didn't think about sunscreen, at all."

Blaire glanced at Bri with shocked eyes and did her best to comfort me. "It isna all that bad, Adelle. It shall heal itself eventually."

"Eventually?" That was not okay with me. It needed to be completely healed by tonight. Once our afternoon of sledding had concluded, Hew had very seriously and nervously asked that I dine with him in the cottage this evening. He said he had something very important he wished to tell me.

"Aye." Blaire sent me a cautious glance.

I knew it wasn't her fault, but she could tell I was agitated by her response that it would take some time for my sunburn to heal.

"I know that 'tis not pleasant for ye, but it shall take at least a week for ye to look like yerself, I'm afraid."

"Awesome." I didn't know what else to say. Nothing could be done for my stupidity. I would look scary when I arrived at the cottage this evening. Perhaps we could dine outside in darkness. Even if we turned into icicles, it would be preferable to frightening the poor man to death with the abomination which was now my face.

"Are ye certain, brother?" Mary asked. "Ye havena been acquainted with Adelle verra long. 'Tis no small decision to decide to leave the home that ye have known for so long."

Hew moved about the cottage nervously. He knew it was a rash decision, but nothing had felt so right to him in a good many years. He loved the lass greatly, and he would tell her so tonight. "Aye, Mary, I am certain. There is naught left for me at home, and there hasna been since the day Mae left me. 'Twas foolish of me to stay there so many years after her death. It pains me to think on all the joy I have missed because I was too frightened to take a chance on being happy again. I wasted much time."

His sister reached out and placed a comforting hand on his

arm. "Nay, brother. Ye dinna waste time. Things happen as they are meant to. If ye truly feel the way ye seem to about Adelle, then I doona believe ye were meant to leave yer home until now. If ye had, it wouldna have been her that ye found."

Mary's words comforted him. She had a kind way of looking at all the mistakes he had made. Regardless, he was thankful he had met Adelle now. "Aye, Mary. I canna imagine not knowing the lass. If I agree to work here at the castle, do ye think that Eoin and Arran shall agree to let me make this cottage my home?"

Mary's laughter made him smile. He should've expected such an answer from his fiery sister. "There is no need for ye to ask either of them," she said. "Ye are welcome to stay here because I say so and that's all the permission ye need. Both of the laddies know it and have since they were bairns. 'Tis I that am truly laird over Conall Castle."

"I believe ye are right, Mary. They all seem to bow at yer feet, regardless of the hard time ye seem to love giving them. Now, allow me to walk ye back to the castle, Lady Laird. I have much to think on. It will take me some time to decide the perfect manner in which to say what I must."

CHAPTER 18

"What in the world is the matter with ye, Adelle?" asked Hew. "Take that covering off the top of yer head."

I knew I looked ridiculous, like I was wearing a cheap Halloween costume with the gauzy fabric over my head, but there was no way I was taking it off. I was a vain woman and not afraid to admit it. Whatever he had to say to me, he could say it to me as I was or not at all. "Sorry. I will do no such thing." I kept my head down, my gaze on the pup in my arms.

Stepping into the cottage, I walked past Hew, setting the growing Bratach on the floor, where he joined Tearlach in their usual game of "who's the toughest brother?"

Hew shut the door to the cottage and walked around to face me, frustration clear in his expression. "Ye look ridiculous, lass. I wish to tell ye something important, and I doona wish to address ye while yer covered like a wee ghost."

I glanced up at him, only barely able to see him through the small holes in the fabric, but I could make out enough of his face to know it was perfectly perfect. Speaking a bit more loudly than might've been necessary to compensate for the fact that the fabric covered my mouth, I said, "How is your face not red as a beet? You were out in the same snow and under the same sun that I was in yesterday, and there is no sign of it anywhere on you!"

He laughed, understanding. "Ach, I see. Did the sun blister yer skin a bit, lass? I should have insisted that ye cover it, but I dinna think of it. I spend much of my days outdoors. I suppose my skin has grown accustomed to such sunlight."

"Well, how wonderful for you. Let's eat." It wasn't only the way my face looked that put me in a sour mood, but the pain from it felt something awful. I'd never been burned so badly in my entire life.

"It shall be mighty hard for ye to eat properly with that cloth covering ye. Just take it off, Adelle. Do ye really think that I'm so concerned with the way yer face looks?"

I nodded emphatically. "Of course you are. All men are."

He rolled his eyes, sat down at the table, and started eating immediately, not waiting for me to join him. "Suit yerself," he responded in between mouthfuls. "But if ye truly believe that, Adelle, ye havena been around the right kind of men. I like yer face verra well, but 'tis not my favorite part of ye."

"Oh, fine. So you're one of those," I said grouchily, unsure why I felt the need to provoke him so.

He gave me a little smirk. "'Tis yer mouth that I was referring to. I enjoy it verra much."

Underneath the veil, my brows met in the center. "My mouth? My lips are quite thin. You have strange tastes."

He stood, and I thought perhaps I had pushed him too far.

"Aye? And ye are a silly lass, Adelle. I dinna mean yer lips. I mean the surprising words that ye always seem to form with them. I have never known a lass so forward."

I looked down, embarrassed. "Yes. I know. That's always been a problem. It's a bit of a turn off, isn't it?"

He frowned once more and came to crouch down next to me, taking my hands into his. "I doona know what ye mean by 'turn off' but, nay, I love the way ye speak verra much. Now, I willna tell ye what I must with that damned cloth covering yer head."

He yanked it away before I could grasp it, then reeled back in disgust, almost falling onto his bottom. "Ach, lass, ye look dreadful. Never ye mind, I doona wish to say what I once wished."

My eyes widened with shock and pain. He quickly scrambled up on his feet to gather me into his arms, laughing softly. "Oh, lass, forgive me. Doona look so upset. I couldna resist it after ye berated me just a moment ago. Ye look mighty fine, lass. Ye always do."

I didn't pull away from him but narrowed my eyes. "No, I do not honestly think I look fine. My face is so red I look like I was born on the sun, and it's quite swollen, as well."

"Doona tell me what I think, lass. I wouldna lie to ye. I doona care if the redness never fades, although it shall. I would still think that ye looked mighty fine. Now, hush. Let me tell ye what I wished to when I asked ye to come here."

I didn't believe a word he said about my face at the moment, but I didn't wish to argue with him anymore. I was eager to hear what he had to say. "All right, fine," I relented. "What is it?"

He stepped away and sat on the edge of the bed, holding my hands so that I would sit next to him. "I've decided that once the snow melts, I am not going to return home."

Hope fluttered in my chest. I'd spent every second trying not to think of the day when he would leave here and praying that the snow would stay forever. "Really? Why?"

"Do ye really not know the answer to that question, lass?"

He looked into my eyes. I could see all that he wished to say deep within them, but I desperately wanted him to speak the words. "Maybe, but I won't know for sure until you tell me."

He took a deep, shaky breath. He was nervous, but I was not about to intervene and let him get away without saying what he felt. I'd let too many men do that before. If he meant it, he could find the strength to say the words. "I...I know that I havena known ye long, Adelle, but it doesna take so long for the heart to know what it wants. I'm in love with ye, lass. Verra much so."

I smiled, staring deep into his eyes. Tears threatened to fall, but I held them back. I must have remained quiet for one moment too long for when he spoke again, his voice was shaky.

"I doona expect that ye should feel the same so quickly. Perhaps 'twas rash for me to tell ye so soon, but I have spent too many years alone. I willna deny myself love a moment longer if I can have it."

"No." I reached up and lay my hand against his cheek. "Hew, no. It wasn't too quickly at all. I love you, too."

"Do ye truly, lass?"

"Yes, I do. I think I loved you the first moment I saw you in the snow, holding that sweet little puppy firm against your chest." I leaned forward and kissed him but had to pull away at the pain that shot through my lips at the pressure.

"Ach, lass. I'm verra sorry that ye are hurting so. Doona kiss me now. I hope there shall be plenty of time for that later."

"There's nothing for you to be sorry about, and yes, I do too."

His face grew serious again, filling my heart with worry for a moment.

"I willna return to where I came from, but before I make this my home, I must finish the journey I started. I must bid Mae farewell one last time, lass. I hope that ye doona mind."

I shook my head, surprised that he thought I might. "Of course I don't, and of course you must. When will you leave?"

He looked out at the snow, hesitating. "At sunrise," he said, finally. "I know that the snow isna melted yet, but no more has fallen in days. I am anxious to finish my journey so I can begin a new chapter in my life."

Something twisted uncomfortably in my stomach, but I could not determine its source and did my best to ignore it. "You will be careful, yes?"

He smiled, rubbing his hand gently up and down my back. "Aye, lass. I will. I have someone most precious to return to now."

I wished to stay with him until morning, but I left shortly after learning he would be taking off at sunrise. I wanted him to be rested before traveling out in the snow. He'd sent both pups with me, entrusting Tearlach to my care for the duration of his journey.

I slept fitfully. While I tossed wildly throughout the night, both pups slept soundly in the bed with me, snuggled tightly to my side. They didn't move all night, only stirring at sunrise. Just as the sun broke over the horizon, they stood on all fours in the bed. Looking toward the window in the direction of the cottage, they whined mournfully.

The knot in my stomach returned.

CHAPTER 19

As planned, Hew left at sunrise. It was not a far journey to Mae's resting place. In fair weather he could have made the trip there and back in a day, but with the snow still so deep, he knew it would take him at least two.

Just two days away from Adelle seemed too many. He wondered if she'd been disappointed that he hadn't asked her to marry him. He hoped she was not, for he intended to do so as soon as he made it back from bidding Mae one final farewell.

He wished to marry Adelle with all his heart, but some small piece of him would not allow himself to ask it of her when Mae still lingered in the back of his mind. He knew his wife would be pleased for him, finding someone to share the rest of his life with, someone he loved. He'd come to that realization soon after he arrived at Conall Castle and met Adelle, but he wished to spend a few moments alone with Mae so that he could truly put the past behind him.

The day trickled by slowly as he lost himself in a sea of past memories. Memories of loneliness and the choices he'd made that had caused him to be so. A new future lay ahead of him. He couldn't wait to embrace it with all that he had.

He stopped often to allow his aging horse to rest and to clean the icy chunks from the horse's hooves and coat. He asked much of his beloved beast to accompany him on this trip. His horse was old. Hew knew the animal would not make it another year. It seemed appropriate that Greggory's last journey be to Mae's grave.

Slowly, dark descended over Hew and the great beast. He knew he should stop for the night, but no good place offered shelter from the snow. There was a small village just outside of the Conalls' territory, so against his better judgment, he nudged the horse on, praying with each soft kick of his heels that his companion could make it into the village.

It happened quickly. The horse stepped upon a rock buried out of sight, deep within the snow. He heard the creature's leg snap and did his best to throw his own leg over the side so that he could dismount before the Greggory fell, but Hew was not quick enough.

The horse fell in the direction Hew dismounted, and Hew's left shoulder dislocated on impact with the frozen ground. He was pinned beneath the injured animal, the weight on top of him squeezing the breath from his lungs.

Pain coursed through him. The stars in the sky melted together, turning into darkness as he lost consciousness.

---

*P*resent Day

"*M*orna...Morna, wake up, lass!" Jerry shook his wife's shoulder with as much force as his thin arms could afford. He watched, terrified, as she tossed in her sleep. The noises she made indicated she was injured. He could see her eyes darting back and forth beneath her closed eyelids, and he held his breath in fear.

"I must gather my spells," she finally said, opening her eyes to look at him. "They are in need of us, Jerry."

He sighed in relief, his whole body trembling from the remnants of his worry. Jerry had often seen his wife stir in discomfort during fitful dreams, but never so much as he'd just witnessed. For a brief moment, he'd worried that it hadn't been magic that caused her to do so, but perhaps old age.

He had every intention of passing from this life before his beloved. He knew he would not be able to live a day without her. "Ye scared me to death, Morna. I was afraid…well, I doona wish to speak of what I thought."

He smiled against her hand as she laid her palm against his cheek, knowing what he meant well enough. "'Tis not a worry ye should have. I shall not leave this world until I am good and ready to, and that willna be for a long time. Come."

She stood and gestured for him to follow her. He did so without question. His wife carried a great burden, one he was eternally grateful he didn't possess. "What is it, lass?"

"A lad I knew as a child has taken a fancy to Adelle, and he finds himself in need of help. I must warn them, send Adelle the dreams that were just shown to me so they may have a chance of reaching him in time."

She didn't stop to explain more to him, and Jerry didn't ask any further questions. This was an urgent matter, but he didn't worry over such things as his wife did. He'd yet to see one of her spells go awry.

CHAPTER 20

I'd slept so little the night before Hew departed that I would have been on edge the next day even if the pups had not chosen the exact moment of his departure to whine as if wounded. I spent the hours after his departure sick with worry, and it exhausted me. My only relief was that my face no longer ached, and the swelling had diminished greatly throughout the day.

As I traveled upstairs to my bedchamber, a pup under each arm, I was sure I would spend another sleepless night worried over Hew. Much to my surprise, a sense of drowsiness so strong that I could barely make it to my bedchamber door without losing consciousness overcame me.

It seemed a great effort to change into my nightgown. As soon as my head hit the pillow, I fell asleep.

I woke in the middle of the night with sweat beaded on my brow. The covers were off of the bed, mangled on the floor as if I had fought a great battle in my sleep. Screaming had pulled me out of the horrific dream I was having, and for a moment I thought I had heard my own yells.

I felt the need to scream now. Visions of Hew crushed beneath the weight of his horse, unable to scoot from beneath the animal, burned in my mind. I stilled in the bed, sitting up so that I could listen.

For a moment all remained quiet, but it took only a second before another scream ripped through the castle corridors.

I leapt out of the bed. Bri. She must have gone into labor sometime in the night. I could only hope that it was just starting, and I had not missed being there for her.

I burst into her and Eoin's bedchamber, relieved to see that Mary was already making preparations, ordering others about while Blaire administered Morna's mixture to Bri.

I ran to my daughter's side, giving her my hand. She squeezed it tightly as a contraction gripped her. "How are you? Is everything well?"

She grunted in between words, her expression set in determination. "Yes, as well as it can be, I believe. Will you go tell Eoin he better get in here this second? I don't care that it's unusual for men to stay at the bedside during delivery during this century. If he misses the birth of his child, I shall never forgive him."

"Of course." I had to pry her fingers loose from my hand. Turning to Mary, I asked, "Is she close, or do we have some time before the baby arrives?"

Mary must have been able to tell something else distressed me for she answered quickly, waving me on to whatever other task sat on my mind. "Nay, she isna as close as she wishes. We have some time still."

I nodded and ran out of the bedchamber, nearly colliding with Eoin, Arran, and Kip, who all huddled together in the hallway. I knew I must do as Bri bid first. Although I was certain my dream had meant something, I couldn't know for sure that what I had seen had been real.

I grabbed Eoin's arm and pulled him away from the circle, smacking him lightly as I scolded him. "What on earth do you think you are doing? You better get in there with Bri right this instant or I am going to drag you there myself."

He looked back at me nervously. "I am afraid to, Adelle. I doona think I can bear to see her in such pain, and I couldna live with the guilt if something happened to her and the babe."

I softened, feeling sorry for him. It was easy for women to forget what a terrifying ordeal childbirth was for the father. "Nothing is going to happen to them. Morna's drink will help with the pain soon and all will go well. Trust me, if you miss this Bri will not understand. Go. Now."

He nodded and hurried down the hall, leaving me to turn my attention to Arran and Kip. "I need to ask something of both of you. I know that you may think me mad, but please I beg you, listen to me before you dismiss me."

Kip stood silently, giving me an expression that I knew meant he dreaded whatever I was about to tell him. He knew it would only mean more work for himself.

Arran nodded and reached out to lay a reassuring hand on my shoulder. "Aye, of course, Adelle. What is it?"

"I had a dream, a terrible one. I've never had one quite so vivid. It was dark, and Hew was lying on his back in the snow. His horse had fallen on top of him, crushing him, and one of his arms hung oddly to his side." Saying what I'd seen out loud made it seem more real to me. As I finished, my voice cracked. I couldn't keep a tear from falling down my face.

Arran glanced quickly at Kip and then back at me. "Do ye think that he is in danger, lass, or did ye only have a dream that has upset ye?"

I shook my head. "I don't know, but I'm afraid that he might be in trouble. I know it seems crazy."

Arran squeezed my shoulder. "Nay, it isna crazy. We have all seen too much of what Morna can do to disregard what might be a warning from her. Kip and I will ride at once."

"Thank you. I'm sorry to send you, but I can't leave Bri right now."

Arran was already moving down the corridor, Kip following silently behind him as he called back to me, "Of course you canna. Doona worry. We shall find him in time."

I believed that they would. They had to. I couldn't bear to think otherwise.

CHAPTER 21

Once Morna's medicine worked its way through Bri's system, her screams lessened substantially and things began moving rather fast.

She dilated more quickly than Mary had expected. Much to her dismay, she was forced to enlist the help of each of us in some way. Blaire did whatever Mary asked of her, while Eoin and I sat on either side of Bri, coaching and calming her with each set of pains.

When it came time for Bri to push, I watched in awe and astonishment at her strength. It was a miraculous thing. The love that filled the room in the moment the tiny bundle arrived into this world was enough for me to momentarily push away my worries over Hew.

While here, there was nothing I could do, and my heart nearly burst through my chest when I held my granddaughter in my arms for the first time.

I'd heard it said before that grandchildren filled you with a kind of love that was not even matched by your children. I'd always thought it a crazy notion, but as I latched on to her tiny fingers, I finally understood.

To hold a little human, one that came from a very piece of me, allowed me for an instant to believe that I would truly live on forever. In Bri, in her daughter, and in whatever children this child would one day have. It was all that one could ask for in life, more than I ever thought I would receive.

"Mom, you're crying more than I am, more than Eoin."

I glanced over to see Eoin practically blubbering in the corner and laughed as I carried the child to Bri's loving arms. "I don't care. I have never seen anything more perfect in my entire life."

Bri smiled, bending to kiss her daughter's head. "I know. Me, either. Where's Arran? I'm sure he's ready to meet his niece."

I didn't wish to burden any of them with bad news, but I knew I must tell them. "It's nothing to worry over I'm sure, but I had a dream about Hew. I became worried that perhaps something had happened to him on his journey. Arran and Kip rode after him to make sure that he is all right."

Bri looked up at me closely, clearly seeing past the calm façade I was doing my best to maintain. "Go."

I shook my head, dismissing her. "No, I'm not going to leave you so soon. You just had a baby, for goodness' sake."

She raised her left hand and shooed me from the room. "Mom, go. Everything is fine here. I know you need to be there. Just promise me you'll be careful."

I couldn't deny she was right. I bent quickly to kiss both her and the babe on the forehead before turning to leave the room. "I will."

I ran to the stables, mounting the first horse I saw, and took off at full speed away from Conall Castle.

CHAPTER 22

I'd left the castle before sunrise, and it neared dusk when I finally found them. The vision before me was just as I'd seen it in the dream. I had been right about Hew. I was certain it was Morna who'd sent the warning to me.

"Is he…" I could hardly force the words out of my mouth. "Is he alive?"

"Aye, lass. I am verra alive and intend to stay that way."

When Hew's voice answered, the relief that washed through me was enough to nearly bring me to my knees.

My legs were shaky as I approached him, the adrenaline that had allowed me to ride to him so quickly suddenly receding. I knelt next to him, grabbing both sides of his face as I examined him for injuries. "Why haven't you moved the horse off of him?" I asked Arran and Kip, who stood behind me. "He's going to lose his legs if the horse stays on him much longer."

"We only just arrived a few minutes before you, lass. Ye must have been riding verra quickly to have caught us."

Hew reached his right hand up to touch my face, his other arm dislocated. "Nay, lass. If I hadna thrown my shoulder out of place, I would have been able to scoot out from under Greggory. I willna lose my legs."

"I'm glad to hear it." I stepped out of the way so that Arran and Kip could get on either side of him. Together they lifted him, avoiding his injured shoulder so that they could pull him out from under the horse, whose breathing was shallow. My heart winced in sadness at the creature's pain. His suffering would have to be ended.

Once Hew's legs were free, Arran had me move to his right side so that I could hold him down and steady while Kip secured his feet. When he was still, Arran asked him to bite down hard on a rag, then he jerked the shoulder into place. It was a horrible sound, but after the initial pain, the relief became instantly visible on Hew's face.

With help, the two men pulled him to his feet, and after a few moments of allowing his blood to circulate, he moved about to get his footing under him.

Eventually, he turned to address all of us. "I am verra grateful for yer help. I hate to ask it of ye, but would ye all mind riding ahead a ways, only for a few moments?"

"Why?" The word slipped out quickly, but as I looked at the way he stared down at his horse, sadness in his eyes, I knew.

"It must be I that end this for him, and I wish to do it alone."

Silently, we turned and left him.

He did not prolong the task. Once Hew joined us, we made plans to stay in the village where he had been headed when his horse had fallen. The village was located close to Mae's grave. Hew was determined to complete the journey he had intended.

Although I couldn't stand the thought of leaving him alone once again, I understood his need to do this one last thing.

*A*rran, Kip, and I had been at the small inn a few hours when Hew arrived. He said little as he entered, only asking which was his room and leaving us in the dining hall to retire for the evening.

We followed him shortly, separating as we each made our way to our rented rooms. We were all exhausted, and I couldn't blame Hew for not wishing to speak with us when he'd arrived. I was just happy to know that he was safe.

He'd suffered much over the last few days. He was sure to be sore, tired, and heartsick at the loss of his beloved horse, not to mention the melancholy I knew he must feel after having visited Mae's grave.

For this reason, I expected it to be Arran or Kip at the door when I heard a soft knock right as I blew out all but the last candle for the evening. Instead, when I opened the door, Hew stood before me.

CHAPTER 23

"You should be in bed. You're injured and it's been a long day."

He didn't answer me, only moved into the room shutting the door behind him. He reached out to me with his good arm, pulling me close to him as he kissed me desperately.

After a moment, he drew back breathlessly. "Doona tell me what I should do, lass. I had to see ye."

He released me, and I stepped away, hoping that putting some distance between us would dim the fire he'd lit within me. "Is everything all right?"

"Aye, lass. Will ye marry me?"

The words caught me off guard. He spoke them so quickly, I wondered for a moment if perhaps he hadn't meant to say them. "What? What did you just say?"

It took him only two strides until he stood before me, clasping tightly onto both of my hands. "Ye did hear me, lass, but I shall ask ye again. Will ye marry me, Adelle?"

A pleading in his eyes nearly broke my heart. After everything, he still worried that I might say no. "Yes, of course."

"Really, ye will, lass?"

"Aye," I said, mimicking his brogue in jest, reaching up to kiss him gently before standing on my tiptoes to whisper into his ear. "I want nothing more than to be your wife."

He kissed me wildly, without restraint. And then we were laughing. Laughing and kissing and holding each other. Now that I'd found him, my soul mate, I never wanted to let go.

Hew didn't leave my room that night, and we didn't take the time to re-light the candles I'd extinguished before he arrived. It didn't matter; the room was ablaze with our love for one another.

CHAPTER 24

We were married in the great room of Conall Castle on New Year's Day, surrounded by all of the people we loved most in the world. The vows were simple, but I'd never meant anything more than the few words we spoke to one another.

Hew's eyes never left mine as I made my promises to him. "I doona know where life will take me, but I choose ye to be at my side. From this day forward, my soul belongs to naught but ye. I now bind myself to ye in the present and for all the times to come. Together we are now one."

I didn't know where the vows came from, and I'd undoubtedly messed up the accent badly, but Hew didn't care, and neither did I.

As he leaned in to kiss me, baby Ellie Adelle Conall, named in honor of Eoin's mother, Elspeth, and myself, squealed as if she'd been pinched. Our pups howled loudly in response.

A happy chaos surrounded us, and it was just as we wished it to be.

I had been right. It had proven to be the best Christmas season that Conall Castle had ever seen.

*T*urn the page for a Sneak Peek of *Morna's Magic* - Book 3.

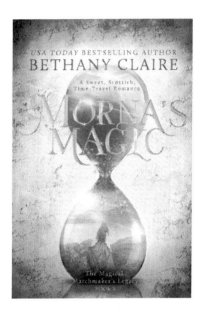

SNEAK PEEK OF MORNA'S MAGIC - BOOK 3

CHAPTER 1

Austin, TX—Present Day

Two thoughts flashed through my mind as my trembling fingers gripped at the letter and the set of keys my husband held out to me. The first was that if Brian said one more word, I planned to take off my shoe and ram the pointy end of the heel deep into his skull. The second was that I was so ashamed of my own stupidity that I was just as inclined to ram the heel of the other shoe into my own head.

How could I have let so many months pass with him making the most ridiculous excuses to stay away from home? How could I not have caught on? What a silly, desperate fool I must be to have made it so easy for him to break his vows. It must've thrilled him to discover he'd married such an unassuming, trusting wife.

Now that I knew what he'd been up to, over a year's worth of clues seemed glaringly obvious. While we'd never truly been happy, I never thought him capable of such a betrayal. He was an ass, but a cheat? A liar? I'd not seen this in him.

I'd had plenty of time to come to terms with his affair. Weeks of lawyer negotiations and packing my belongings had quickly made me glad to be rid of him. But what had me shaking with anger and unshed tears was the revelation I held in my hand.

"Are you really so surprised, Mitsy?" Brian said defensively. "Bri left too quickly to sell the place, and it's not like she had that many friends. She left it in your care so why shouldn't I have used her house? What did it hurt?"

I squeezed the key so tightly that its ridges buried deep into my hand, indenting the skin. I was sure he could see the steam coming out of my ears, but I refused to scream at him as he expected me to. Brian would call it another one of my "ginger" moments and use it as justification for the affair. I would not give him the satisfaction.

"No." I said the word calmly and slowly released my breath so that it didn't come out as a loud sigh of frustration. "I'm not surprised she left me the house, I'd just never given it much thought. What I'm surprised about is how you thought it was okay to keep this letter from me. This is not addressed to you."

He chuckled, and I ground my heel into the floor to keep myself from ripping it off and attacking him.

"You're right. It isn't, but we were married when it came in the mail and what's yours is mine, yes? Besides, Leah and I needed somewhere to go. It's not like we could come back here when you were always sitting in the house waiting on me."

My face could not have grown any hotter, but still I did not raise my voice. "You can justify anything, can't you? Bri would strangle you herself if she knew you'd been using her house to cheat on me."

Turning from him, I walked across the room to swing the last of my belongings, all thrown messily into a large duffle bag, over my shoulder so that I could make my way out the door. I'd not even read the letter yet. As soon as I saw Bri Conall's handwriting and the key tucked inside the envelope, I knew that my friend had left her house in my care. The date at the top showed just how long Brian had kept this from me.

There was so much more that I could say to him, so much more I wanted to say, but I knew none of it would do any good. He would never see anything wrong with the kind of man he was, and I was tired of him. I was tired of everything, really. I only wanted to get out of this house without saying another word. I didn't ever want to see him again.

"I wasn't the only one who cheated," Brian said behind me. "Maybe you didn't do it physically, but in your mind you did. Every time I held you, I could see *him* behind your eyes. It's too bad for you, really. He didn't want you, either. That's why you ran to me, isn't it?"

I didn't respond. If only Brian would let me be and not say anything else, I might be able to make it out of the room and to my car without bursting into tears. But I knew he wouldn't be so kind.

"Bri is nuts," he continued. "She rambles on in the letter about you coming to visit her at the castle and how much you would love the seventeenth century. Bri's completely out of her mind. No wonder you two were such good friends."

I kept my back to him as I reached for the door handle, and I swallowed the lump in my throat when he chuckled again. "Goodbye, Brian." I didn't look back as I walked out the door, climbed into my car and started the engine, then pulled out of the driveway.

In the rearview mirror I saw Brian's mistress, Leah, pulling into the spot I'd just deserted, replacing me so quickly at our home it was as if I'd never been there. I couldn't bring myself to feel any hatred toward her. Only pity. God help her, the poor girl had no idea what she'd gotten herself into.

As much as I didn't want to spend the night at Bri's old house, especially after learning what Brian had used it for, I was relieved to cancel my hotel reservations. Classroom teachers don't make much money, and as a teacher's aide, I made even less. I couldn't move into my new apartment for another week, and with no family to offer me shelter until then, I had no choice but to reserve a room at the shabbiest of hotels.

If it meant saving a little money, I could push away the memories that would flood over me at Bri's—Brian's love nest. Memories of nights spent with Brian there when it had been his and we'd been dating, before he sold the house to my friend. Memories of helping Bri paint and refurbish the old bachelor pad until it was beautiful and perfect, just as she wished it. It's not as if I planned on sleeping much anyway.

The flowers on the front porch that she once tended so carefully had long since died, and an uncomfortable pang knocked on my heart at the thought of how much I missed Bri. I still didn't fully understand what had happened to her. She was the classroom teacher, and I worked directly under her. She was also the closest friend I'd ever had. When she disappeared after accompanying her archaeologist mother on a dig in Scotland, it's no stretch to say that I lost it a little.

When I finally found her after flying to Scotland, it was clear that she'd fallen madly in love. I saw how much her new husband, Eoin, adored her, and I couldn't blame her a bit for leaving everything behind. I would've done the same.

I'd experienced love like that once, but it hadn't been with

Brian. What he'd said to me was true. The loss of Jep—the man I'd loved—led me to settle for Brian.

I understood Bri when it came to the love thing. What I didn't understand was why she'd lied to me about it. She had lied so confidently, weaving a story so detailed that I truly did want to believe it, but I couldn't. People do not—and she did not—travel through time.

Anxious to read her letter, I turned the key and stepped inside the entryway. To my surprise, the place was immaculate. Well, at least the front part of the house was. Most likely only one area of the house had been regularly used, and I would stay clear of that room.

I dropped my bag in the doorway, carrying only the letter into the living room with me as I slowly made my way around the space, turning on lamps and lighting a few candles.

Once the room was properly lit and the smell of pumpkin-scented candles wafted sweetly through the air, I went into the kitchen and put a kettle of water on the stovetop to heat, preparing to steep a large cup of tea. I was in desperate need of something to soothe my frazzled nerves and angry heart.

It had been weeks since I'd slept properly. Now that the divorce was final and Brian was out of my life, all of the stress, sadness, anxiety, and insomnia of the past weeks seemed to hit me at once.

After the kettle whistled and I poured the steaming water over a large cup filled with several tea bags, I all but collapsed onto the oversized sofa that sat in the middle of the living room. I found a coaster and set my tea cup on it, then propped the pillows up behind me so that I could sit comfortably while reading Bri's letter.

I was incredibly curious to do so. I'd not heard a word from her since the wedding. She'd not even taken the time to say goodbye, slipping away during the middle of the reception. I was still angry about that, but I supposed Bri had her reasons. And she did leave me a house, which certainly counted for something. Not that she could've known just how much I would need it. Or perhaps she had, and that was the very reason she had left it for me. Bri had never really liked Brian.

I didn't need to open the envelope. Brian had already done that, and the rumpled edges showed just how many times he'd read through it himself, clearly trying to make sense of Bri's words.

The letter was short and the handwriting definitely Bri's, although it looked hurried. Something told me her idea to write the letter had been a last minute thought before she returned to Scotland. The first part was what I'd expected—an apology for leaving so suddenly and an explanation that the house was now mine to use as I saw fit. She spoke of how much she loved me, how much my friendship meant to her. Then she launched into what Brian had mentioned, speaking of her love of life in the seventeenth century and suggesting I might love it, too.

After that, she changed subjects quickly, only writing a few sentences at the bottom of the page. She'd not even bothered to sign her name.

"The house is yours while you need it, Mitsy, but when it comes time for you to get away and you're ready to start a new life, come and find me. You're welcome here. You will need the help of the innkeepers you met in Scotland. I'm not going to bother trying to tell you what happened again. I know you didn't believe me last time, and I don't expect you will believe me now...not until you experience it. Call them when you're ready."

Staring down at the odd message with fascination, I flung my feet over the edge of the couch, suddenly needing a large gulp of tea. Bri's statement was written as if she knew that I would want to leave here one day, that I would want to leave Brian. There was no *if* in her hastily scribbled message. Not only that, it suddenly seemed to me that perhaps she didn't intentionally lie about time traveling back to the seventeenth century. Bri actually believed she'd done just that.

Which changed things and made me worry for her all the more. Even after I found Bri and she told me the elaborate tale, even after I met Blaire, the woman who so closely resembled her that I was certain they had to be related in some manner, I still could not believe my friend's story. There was a reason she felt the need to lie. Frankly, I was so glad to know that Bri was alive and not murdered, buried in a ditch in the middle of Scotland, that I had decided to let it go. Begrudgingly, I'd accepted the fact that I might never know the truth of what happened to her after she disappeared. But if Bri truly believed that she'd traveled back in time, then something terrible must've happened to her.

Her brain was addled, disturbed, and I owed it to her to find out just what and who had done this to her. Not that I didn't need to get away from this place for personal reasons – I certainly did. But a trip to Scotland to find Bri and try to talk her out of her delusions would be the perfect excuse to leave. Better to help someone else out of a problem than to wade in the self-pity I felt at my own.

Making my way back to the front doorway, I found my duffle bag and withdrew my wallet and cell phone. I recalled writing down the phone number for the strange innkeepers I met the last time I searched for Bri. The old couple had been nearly impossible to reach, and I was not altogether sure that I'd be able to make contact with them again. I got the impression that their phone number and address were not readily available.

Finding the slip of paper in my wallet, I clicked the call button on my phone and punched in the number as quickly as I could, not waiting a moment so that I could change my mind. The phone rang once and then was answered by the unmistakable voice of the innkeeper herself.

"Why, Mitsy, how are ye, dear? Jerry and I have been expecting a call from ye any minute. I suggest that ye start packing up yer things, though ye willna need much once ye get here."

My mouth hung open. How did she know it was me who'd called? I doubted that she had caller ID at the little inn. How did she know that I planned on coming there? I'd yet to say a word to her, and I didn't know what to say now. "Um...hi. Why would you expect a call from me?"

The old woman at the other end of the phone laughed softly. "Well, dear, I know a large number of things that I doubt ye would expect me to. Best ye get yerself here and then I will tell ye more. I'm sure ye willna believe a bit of it, though, until ye see it for yerself."

She was certainly right about that. "Ok...uh, is Bri there? May I speak to her for a moment?"

I knew she would tell me Bri wasn't there, but obviously she was. How else would the woman have known that Bri suggested I come there?

"Ye know that she isna here, love. She's a far time away from here to be sure, but ye will see her soon enough. She told me to tell ye when ye called that she doesna wish for ye to pay for yer plane ticket on yer own. She knows your budget is limited. I've already called the airline and purchased a ticket for ye. Yer flight is at 3:00 p.m. tomorrow. All ye need to do is check in at the counter. Yer rental car has been arranged, as well. I suppose since ye found yer way to our inn once before, ye are capable of doing so again. We will see ye soon. Safe travels, Mitsy."

She hung up the phone, and I stared at the wall in confusion. Thank God it was summer. As long as I didn't stay gone for more than a month, I wouldn't have to make arrangements at work.

It seemed that by this time tomorrow, I would find myself on a flight headed to Scotland.

Get *Morna's Magic* - **Book 3** to continue reading the rest of the story.

Morna's Magic
(The Magical Matchmaker's Legacy - Book 3)

BOOKS IN THE MAGICAL MATCHMAKER'S LEGACY

Morna's Spell - Book 1

Morna's Secret - Book 2

The Conall's Magical Yuletide - Book 2.5

Morna's Magic - Book 3

Morna's Accomplice - Book 4

Jeffrey's Only Wish - Book 4.5

Morna's Rogue - Book 5

Morna's Ghost - Book 6

Morna's Vow - Book 7

The McMillan's Magical Yuletide - Book 7.5

Morna's Turn - Book 8

LETTER TO READERS

Dear Reader,

I hope you enjoyed *The Conall's Magical Yuletide (The Magical Matchmaker's Legacy - Book 2.5)*. I hope you continue with *Morna's Magic - Book 3*.

As an author, I love feedback from readers. You are the reason that I write, and I love hearing from you. If you would like to connect, there are several ways you can do so. You can reach out to me on Facebook or on Twitter or visit my Pinterest boards. If you want to read excerpts from my books, listen to audiobook samples, learn more about me, and find some cool downloadable files related to the books, visit my website.

The best way to stay in touch is to subscribe to my newsletter. Go to my website and subscribe in the box in the middle of the page under "Newsletter" that asks for your email address or submit your email address. If you don't hear from me regularly, please check your spam folder or junk mail to make sure my messages aren't ending up there. Please set up your email to allow my messages through to you so you never miss a new book, a chance to win great prizes or a possible appearance in your area.

Finally, if you enjoyed this book, I would appreciate it so much if you would recommend it to your friends and family. And if you would please take time to review it on Goodreads and/or your favorite retailer site, it would be a great help. Reviews can be tough to come by these days, and you, the reader, have the power to make or break a book.

Thank you so much for reading my books. I hope you choose to journey with me through the other books in the series.

All my best,
   Bethany

ABOUT THE AUTHOR

BETHANY CLAIRE is a USA Today bestselling author of swoonworthy, Scottish romance and time travel novels. Bethany loves to immerse her readers in worlds filled with lush landscapes, hunky Scots, lots of magic, and happy endings.

She has two ornery fur-babies, plays the piano every day, and loves Disney and yoga pants more than any twenty-something really should. She is most creative after a good night's sleep and the perfect cup of tea. When not writing, Bethany travels as much as she possibly can, and she never leaves home without a good book to keep her company.

In addition to writing, Bethany is also a sought after self-publishing instructor and advisor who has helped many writers develop a road map to help them succeed in Indie publishing. She is the co-founder of www.masteringselfpublishing.com, a site dedicated to helping Indies create thriving publishing businesses by offering educational resources through online courses and consultations.

If you want to read more about Bethany or if you're curious about when her next book will come out, please visit her website at: www.bethanyclaire.com, where you can sign up to receive email notifications about new releases.

Connect with Bethany on social media, visit her website for lots of book extras, or email her:

www.bethanyclaire.com
bclaire@bethanyclaire.com

ACKNOWLEDGMENTS

I love Christmas, so even though this book didn't have nearly as much to clean up as the other books in my series, I still wanted this novella to be included in the "sweet" editions. As with every book, there are so many people that contribute, and for them I am so thankful.

J.J. Archer – thanks so much for another stellar project.

Karen Corboy, Elizabeth Halliday, and Johnetta Ivey, thanks so much for your keen eyes and suggestions.

Mom, I know these rewrites meant that you had to read all of these books again which means you're probably on like your 20th read now. Even I don't want to read them that many times. Thanks for all you do.

Printed in Great Britain
by Amazon